MURDER IN A DARK GLOOM

A PARKER PHOTOGRAPHY COZY MYSTERY

SUZANNE BOLDEN

LAUGHING DEER PRESS

Published by Laughing Deer Press

Cover design Molly Burton www.cozycoverdesigns.com

CONTENTS

CHAPTER ONE

"This is quite the soiree," my Aunt Ruth said as we turned into the long drive and approached Harmony House on its perch above the river.

"Think they'll have a red carpet rolled out for us?" I teased.

"Well, they might. I heard there will be a senator in attendance, and someone said the press from Milwaukee will even be here," Ruth said. "Stuart Walters will be in hog heaven writing this up for our local paper."

"It'll be good to see him again." I pulled up in front of the mansion to drop Ruth off. Up lighting thrown against the tall sturdy oaks was magical. Luminaries glowed on the walkway to the front porch.

This fundraiser was a big event for the little village of Harmony. My memories of only a few months ago flooded back. I hoped to see Eleanor Harmony tonight. The last time I'd been with her had not been pleasant for either of us. This would be quite a different scene.

Ruth looked lovely in her formal gown. I sensed her excitement. She and her friends at Shady Pines had decided to pull out all the punches to attend this once in a decade event. They were making the most of it! Dorothy's granddaughter had piled them all in her minivan, and they traveled together to a dress shop in Madison to find evening wear. Then today, they spent time together at Val's Cut-n-Curl for manicures, pedicures, and hairstyling. Wish I could have been a fly on the wall there.

"I'll park and be right up. You go on ahead," I said as Ruth stepped out and adjusted her dress. "By the way, did I tell you how gorgeous you look?"

She grinned at me and did a twirl on the sidewalk. "Old lady still has it." She walked off with an extra wiggle of her behind. Spunky for an octogenarian. I hope I inherited some of that through my Parker family genes.

I turned my SUV's wheels to pull back out when a loud honk alerted me to the fact that a car had pulled up right next to me.

"Okay. Okay. Didn't see you," I mumbled as I waited for them to move. In my side mirror I saw a foot in a high heeled red shoe emerge from the rear car door, followed by a long leg peeking out of the slit in an elegant red gown. The passenger stood and paused to collect herself, surveying the scene before taking the arm of a man who'd been waiting to greet her. They air kissed as the car she'd arrived in began to pull away.

The chauffeur nodded at me as he drove past. This was more than a little historical society fundraiser. One never saw chauffeured cars around Harmony unless it was a wedding party being driven between the church and the ballroom.

In my business as a photographer, I've attended many formal events, not only in Chicago where I live, but around the world. I was glad I'd chosen my long satin navy-blue skirt, instead of the calf length black one I'd also packed. I tended to dress to blend in, not stand out like the woman in the red gown. But that kind of person always did add a bit of spice to a party.

The people of Harmony were surprised, but excited, when Eleanor Harmony, after losing her fiancé on the eve of their wedding, decided to donate her family mansion to the village and move into the smaller home where her parents had been raised. Downsizing, she called it. Eleanor was closer to Aunt Ruth's age, but even me, in my 60s, could understand the sense of that move.

The Historical Society outdid themselves with this fundraiser to get the mansion and grounds up to modern-day standards. Ruth had been telling me about all the hard work put into making this evening special. And their efforts obviously paid off.

Familiar faces greeted me as I entered. Hannah and her husband Mark, owners of the local antique shop, waved from the top of the grand staircase. Ruth told me they had been hired to catalog and appraise the antiques here. My lifelong friend, Wanda Mathis, took a champagne glass from a waiter's tray. She gave me an okay finger circle and quick point toward the champagne glasses still on the tray. I nodded and watched her smoothly grab another glass and head over to me.

"Jackie!"

I spun to see who had screamed my name. Hurrying toward me was a vision in another stunning red gown, with her thick chestnut hair piled up in an intricately woven crown on top of her head. Kim Walters, local real estate agent extraordinaire, practically jumped into my arms. Luckily, I braced myself.

"You did come! Hooray! I'm so happy. When I noticed you donated a portrait sitting to the silent auction, I just knew I'd be bidding on that one. I mean, who wouldn't want to sit for such a famous photographer? Do you believe the turnout for this gala?" She spun around, throwing her hands in the air. "Why everyone who is anyone is here!"

She hadn't changed. And tonight, she was in her element. Kim was the go-to realtor for Harmony. A reputation she deserved and made well known to anyone within earshot.

"You look gorgeous, Kim. That rich red color is perfect for you. Is your husband Stuart here?"

She looked around the room. "Hmm…he's here somewhere doing his newspaper thing. It'll be a bigger edition on this Tuesday. Harmony hasn't seen an event like this in a long time. And I'm just so glad to be a part of it. I donated the pamphlets explaining the vision for Harmony House."

"That's very generous of you," I said. "I'll have to be sure to pick one up."

Kim reached inside her evening bag. "Oh darn, I don't have anymore. But they're spread around all over. I had your Aunt Ruth do new headshots of me for my ad on the back. Have to stay current. Will you look at her!"

Kim took my shoulder and forced me to look toward the parlor area.

"Who, Kim?" I asked, praying Wanda would get here soon and rescue me.

"Luella Hagge, in a red dress almost identical to mine. I could wring her neck," Kim said through gritted teeth.

It was the woman from the limo. "Kim," I said, extracting myself from her grasp. "It really doesn't look much like yours. Besides, you wear red much better than she does."

The remark calmed her down. "Thank you, Jackie. That compliment means a great deal. In fact, I traveled to your stomping grounds in Chicago to find just the right dress for this evening. You look lovely as well... Vera Wang? Oh, and guess what? Alan Morris is going to be here. Remember him? He's still involved with the land deal for the resort." Kim took a breath to straighten her shoulders and stretched her neck up to search over the crowd. "I must make sure to catch up with him."

I saw a chance to make my break. "If you'll excuse me, Kim, I see a glass of champagne with my name on it."

She touched my arm and in a soft conspiratorial voice said, "I'm glad I solved the mystery of Paul's death with you. What a tragedy. And to think, I provided the final link so the arrest could be made."

She waited, obviously expecting appreciative recognition from me.

"It was a tragedy. I'm sure Eleanor appreciates your contribution to the investigation."

With a smug smile, she licked her lips and said, "Oh, and I hope you find Stu. See you later. I have to go make that bid on your donation!"

Wanda almost crashed into another guest as she made her way across the room. The older gentleman was light on his feet as he shuffled easily sideways and pulled his body out of her way to avoid a collision. Wanda flushed, acknowledging him with her open smile and an oops grimace. I watched them exchange a few words.

"Whew, that was close," she said, handing me a crystal champagne glass filled with bubbly and simultaneously raising hers for a toast. "Welcome back home, my friend. May Harmony's Historical Society rake in piles of dough tonight."

"This is amazing. Aunt Ruth told me how hard the committee has been working to pull this together."

"With a good haul tonight, they can get the place up and running soon. Have you seen the renderings of the proposed changes?" Wanda said.

"No, I haven't. Just got here. I dropped Aunt Ruth off before I parked, and I've already lost her."

"I saw you run into Kim. You'll see her mug plastered

all over the handouts she donated. But thankfully the renderings are a Kim free zone."

I followed Wanda. She wasn't easy to lose. Her typical style of choosing vivid colors and prints made her dress stand out in this crowd. Across the room, Scott Drake stood by three tripod display stands with proposed updates to the house and grounds exhibited on them. He pointed at specific items and seemed to be explaining them to the woman from the limo. Luella Hagge hung on his every word. She practically leaned on him as she listened intently.

Wanda explained to me how they had plans to rent out the mansion and grounds for events and have an area for school and scout groups to experience nature. "Eleanor has to be happy about her decision. Something like this is a once in a lifetime chance for a small village like Harmony to preserve and display its history."

Scott caught Wanda's eye and gave a wink. Luella noticed it and turned to glance at us before giving us a beauty pageant smile.

"It's a big deal. Lots of volunteers will be helping get the place ready," Wanda said.

"Is Drake Construction involved in the project?"

"Yes. Scott's been instrumental in pushing it forward. Eleanor didn't want to donate something to the society that needed a lot of updating, so Scott has been upgrading plumbing and electrical. The society committee chose to keep him on to complete changes for them. Want to rescue him? Looks like he's stuck with Luella."

I'd met Scott Drake the last time I visited and found him very personable and easy on the eyes. And with that low, slow Sam Elliott voice, a joy to listen to. His daughter-in-law, Mandy Drake, was doing a great job working with my aunt in the Parker Photography studio. In fact, I needed to keep an eye out for her because I wanted to ask her something.

"Who is this Luella person? I noticed her arriving in a limousine," I whispered to Wanda.

"Of course, she would make an entrance like that. She likes attention. Like how her red gown screams *look at me*. Luella is the current head of the county's Building and Zoning Department. But she's running for DA against Len Lampert in a special election. Looks like she's campaigning hard for Scott's vote," Wanda said in a suggestive voice.

I didn't have to be asked twice to be part of this rescue mission. We wound our way through the crowd.

CHAPTER TWO

Scott Drake welcomed Wanda with a quick hug, purposely maneuvering himself to end up as far away from Luella as he could. He greeted me with a handshake. Did he even remember me?

"Luella Hagge, may I introduce Wanda Mathis, owner of the charming Riverview Motel? And Jacqueline Parker, professional photographer and native daughter of Harmony."

He remembered me. I was glad.

"Nice to meet you, ladies." Luella reached out with a firm handshake. "Have you seen these wonderful plans? Scott was explaining them to me, and I'm very impressed. I imagine all the permits and zoning approvals will be easily met. Scott is such a professional.

Believe me, not all presentations that come before me are this well done."

"I really appreciate that, especially coming from you," Scott said.

Luella pulled a business card out of her slim evening bag. "I look forward to discussing this with you later. I'd best mingle and meet my constituents."

When she stepped out of earshot, Scott said, "She sure doesn't look like any county department head I've seen. But I have heard of her operations being equated with the wild west days…money under the table, permit applications disappearing, inspectors getting fired. Any way, it's great to see you again, Jackie. Are you in town for very long?"

"A few days. I have some things to take care of, and my Aunt Ruth might need help with something requiring your services. I'll give you a call if that's okay."

"Sure. Love to help her out."

Wanda reached for another champagne glass from a passing waiter and handed it to Scott, but he waved her offer off. "Thanks, but I'm heading to the bar for a beer. I'll be stopping at the auction table to bid on a couple of things."

"More for me," Wanda said with a happy shrug, holding the full champagne flute at her side. "I'm on my way there too, but I'm going for more raffle tickets. Did you see the prizes?"

"Like the weekend stay at the best cabin the Riverview has to offer. Yes, I did," Scott said with a wink. "And I've already bought thirty raffle tickets. But thought I'd do a write-in bid on a certain photographer's auction donation."

Hannah Sutton joined us just as Wanda said, "I'm hoping to win the VIP passes to Taliesin. I haven't been there in years. The committee is researching and working with the non-profit there to learn how they do it so well."

"We are receiving lots of welcome input from them," Hannah said. "Lessons learned about running an estate and home open to the public. All the tour stuff, like crowd control and ways to manage the finances. We have a great deal to learn."

Taliesin, the home and school of Frank Lloyd Wright, was just a few miles away and I would imagine had a much bigger international draw than Harmony House and Museum will ever have, but who was I to burst Hannah's bubble?

Wanda, as usual, had something to add. "Hannah, for god's sake. Do you really think this Harmony Museum will have to deal with issues of crowd control?"

Hannah burst out laughing. "I guess I am going overboard a little. I just love that we are going to pull this off. Donations have been coming in strong. Mark and I are swamped with the antiques and rare items here. It's been amazing what the Harmony family acquired!"

Across the room, I caught a glimpse of Aunt Ruth with her friends, Dorothy, Eunice, and Betty. One of my reasons for coming here for this visit, besides supporting the efforts of the Historical Society, was to see to it that my Aunt Ruth could enjoy the rest of her life with her friends at Shady Pines. Watching them all dolled up and enjoying their evening affirmed the decisions I'd made. Now fingers crossed, I could convince her I was right.

The man who'd almost bumped into Wanda was entertaining the gals. In fact, as I watched, he reached for Betty's hand and led her to an empty space in front of the small combo playing *In the Mood,* the song made famous by Glenn Miller. The two of them did a terrific job with their swing dance moves. When the song finished, he pulled off a smooth dip, leaving Betty giggling and the crowd clapping.

Hannah noticed the dance, too. "He looks like a fun guy. I'm so glad to see them enjoying themselves. Did you know all of them were working with the committee to set this event up? All hands on deck. This was our biggest undertaking."

"And looks like it's going smoothly," I said.

"Jackie, I meant to thank you personally for your donation of a photography sitting to the silent auction," Hannah said.

"My pleasure. You mentioned being swamped with the antiques here. Will you be keeping them for display in the house?" I asked.

"We will be using many of them to do historically accurate stagings of the rooms," Hannah said. "There are literally hundreds of pieces of furniture, bric-à-brac, china, and linens. Eleanor's leaving so much. You should see what all's in the attic. Of course, she's taking some things from here to the Mill House."

A wicked little chuckle escaped Wanda. "Including Tom, I understand."

I exclaimed, "What? Tom and Eleanor? That's wonderful news." Tom had been an employee of the Harmony family for decades. He adored Eleanor Harmony and saw her through three marriages and almost a fourth one. This was a perfect romantic ending for the two of them.

Hannah laughed. "It caught a lot of people by surprise, Jackie. But they were married by their pastor, and it's all on the up and up. Oh, and I just thought of something I wanted to show you. Some articles of clothing upstairs have labels from your mother's dress shop sewn in them!"

"Seriously? I didn't know that was even done."

My last time in Harmony, I peeked inside the old place, now Sutton's Antiques, which long ago had been my mother's dress shop…Vogue on Main. I never really appreciated what a presence that place had. I'd always been much more interested in what my father and his sister Ruth did at Parker Photography.

Memories came rushing back. Dressing rooms elegantly appointed with long mirrors and tufted velvet chairs. Platforms where women stood patiently while a seamstress made alterations or pinned up a hem. How the idealized and unbending mannequin bodies unnerved me with their blank stares.

"I would love to look at those garments. Can we slip away for a moment and take a peek?"

"Sure, I don't see why not. We'd have to go up to the attic. Come on, we'll sneak through the kitchen to the back staircase," Hannah said. "Wanda, you want to come along?"

"Back staircase? Attic? That equals too much climbing in high heels for this woman," Wanda said, rolling first one ankle, then the other.

I said, "Take 'em off. I have memories of you at our

prom ending up in bare feet slow dancing with John to *The First Time Ever I Saw Your Face.*"

"And you, my friend, with that Farrah Fawcett hair, were doing the same with Jack," Wanda retorted. "I loved Roberta Flack. I still play her music. And yes, I did take my shoes off. But if I do that now to climb those stairs, I won't get them back on. As the proprietor of the Riverview Motel and Cabins, I have an image to maintain."

"True. At least in public," I said.

Stuart Walters, Kim's husband, walked up with a big hello for me. He ran the entire operation at the Harmony Hills Happenings, a twice weekly newspaper that was still printed on real paper. "Isn't this quite an event?" he gushed. "Hannah dear, could I steal you away for a photograph by the renderings? It'll make an eye-catching front-page photo in Tuesday's edition."

"Sorry, Jackie. Give me a minute with Stu. I'll meet you in the kitchen in ten," Hannah said, taking Stu by the elbow.

Wanda said, "And I'm making my way to the raffle table…Taliesin, here I come!"

I decided to explore a little more. At this point, I'd barely made it beyond the oversized hallway, which was filled with guests milling about. I headed toward the solarium, where a small combo played. The wicker furniture and oversize ferns, ficus trees, and colorful sprays of orchids hugged the borders of the room, clearing an area for mingling and dancing.

I couldn't resist stepping outside and looking up at the star filled night. In Chicago, where I live in a loft condo, such visibility of the night sky was impossible. Too much light pollution there. But here the full moon, like a giant floodlight, illuminated the trees, shrubs, and flower beds, bathing them in a soft silvery glow. I looked across the lawn where the wedding of Paul and Eleanor was to have occurred. To think of all the people and things that had walked over these grounds. Such a history.

"Lost in thought?"

Startled, I gasped.

"Didn't mean to frighten you," a man standing in the shadows said. "I stepped outside to enjoy a cigar in peace and quiet."

I squinted, trying to make out his face. It was the man Betty had been dancing with. He stepped forward where I could see him. He was a short man, but his carriage made him seem taller. His tuxedo, hand tailored, fit his small frame perfectly. Not handsome in the rugged way Scott Drake was, but attractive because he exuded self-confidence and ease.

"I was caught up in the beauty of the evening," I said.

"Yes, it is that kind of night. Enjoy." He nodded and walked away, the scent of his cigar lingering in the night air. I've always appreciated the smell of a good cigar.

I strolled further, wanting to look back at the mansion. The glass walls of the solarium revealed the colorful revelers as if on a stage. Guests sat at the outside patio tables. Candles flickered in hurricane glasses.

I moved further across the lawns. All the first-floor windows were lit. Between the wooden mullions of the panes, I watched figures moving about inside. Heavy limestone trim framed the windows, giving a sense of sturdiness many modern homes lacked.

My eyes, adjusting to the darkness, discovered a solidly built, vine-covered trellis tucked away in a small, hidden corner. It rose up to the second story, where very few lights were on.

I'd better get back inside. Hannah might be waiting for me.

Crossing back towards the solarium, I noticed a lone figure pacing in one of the first-floor rooms. If I remembered correctly, that was the office of Eleanor's father. The person had an irregular, aggressive gait. That might be Alan Morris. I recall he had a slight limp, and Kim said he was expected to be here. She'll be happy he showed up.

There must be someone else in the room, as he stopped and appeared to be talking. A flash of red suddenly moved past the man and out of sight.

A chill in the air descended over the landscape. I shivered as I hurried back inside.

CHAPTER THREE

In the kitchen, things were bustling. I hung back near the staircase until I saw Hannah arrive. She stopped to say hello to Grace and Dermot Murphy, the local coffee shop owners, who appeared to be serving dessert. I made a mental note to get one of their donuts before the night was over.

A waiter pushing through the door shouted, "Clean up in the parlor!" He headed to an efficient, no muss, no fuss looking woman. "And I'll need your business card, Darlene. Cleaning the champagne out of that fancy red dress is going to cost a pretty penny."

The woman barely missed a beat. "Here's my card. So, one of our staff caused this?"

"Didn't look like it to me. She's raising a ruckus over

it. Not much got on her dress, but I wouldn't argue with her, not worth it," the waiter said.

"Please make proper apologies for us. Glass breakage as well?" Darlene said.

"Just one glass. I'll be sure to take care of it."

Hannah overheard the conversation, too. "Darlene's a pro with her catering business. Nothing she can't handle. I've never seen her get rattled."

"Want to place a bet on who the woman in the red dress is? Kim or Luella?" I asked.

"I'd say it's a coin toss. But I'll go with Luella for a glass of Cabernet," Hannah said.

"I'll take that bet. Ready to head upstairs?" I hiked up my long skirt to make the climb up the narrow staircase.

Back staircases were common in the homes of the wealthy during the early 1900s. They were used primarily by the household staff to move about the mansion without carrying linens and cleaning supplies up the main staircase. This one made a few bends and turns on our way up to the third floor. Finally reaching the top, I was surprised to see the long hallway we had entered.

"This doesn't look like a typical attic, Hannah."

"I used that term loosely. Most of this floor is under the roof slope like attics are." She opened one of the many doors lining the hall. "Notice how the window is in a dormer and the wall meets the slope of the ceiling?"

Through the dormer window, the full moon illuminated a simple white iron bed and an old pine dresser. A straight-back chair with a woven cane seat sat in the corner. A bundle of folded linens lay on the bare mattress, and a small carpet was rolled up on the floor next to it.

"Eleanor has a treasure trove of information about her family. She explained how they often hired young local girls, usually from the surrounding farms, to help with household chores, like cleaning and laundry. They'd stay in these rooms, so they didn't have to make the long trek back and forth every day."

"Will this floor be open for tours eventually, too?" I asked.

"That's the plan. But probably not for several months. Besides the staff bedrooms, many of these rooms were used as storage for out of season clothing and seasonal decor items."

She led us to the far end of the hall, opening the door to an expansive room. "Here we are."

The space had simple unfinished plank floors, exposed rafters, and typical nostalgic things that, as children, we believed lived in everyone's grandmother's attic. Old leather trunks with heavy locks and thick strapping held mysterious post cards from exotic lands. A creepy dress form stood in a dark corner. Heavy ornate frames with old family portraits leaned against the sloping eaves.

"This looks like an illustration from a children's book," I said.

"I know, right? This entire floor was frozen in time. And we've already gotten the big furniture pieces out. Now you see what I mean about the job ahead of us. Here is the wardrobe with the garments labeled as being from your mother's dress shop."

I touched the garments. Things my mother touched. The scent of her Tabu perfume floated across time to me. I heard her humming some current tune, like *In the Still of the Night* or *Mack the Knife,* under her breath as she basted an alteration in place to be stitched and delivered to a customer in the morning. I remembered her smile as I walked in after school to say hello.

"You look lost in thought," Hannah said. "I hope seeing these didn't upset you?"

"Just caught up in the memories," I said.

"You're welcome to come up here anytime, but I'd better get back to the party. I'll show you my office," Hannah said. "I need to pick up something I promised one of the guests."

We returned to the far end of the hall and the back

staircase. But instead of making our way down two flights, we went down only one and opened the door to the second floor.

A woman stood there with a comical, startled reaction. "Oh goodness, you scared me!" A nervous, flustered laugh followed. "I'm afraid I'm a bit turned around here. Ah, I was looking for the powder room."

"So sorry, Betsy. Do you remember me? Hannah from Sutton Antiques."

"You have that shop on Main Street in Harmony, don't you?"

"I do. You've purchased several pieces from me. This is my friend Jacqueline Parker."

"The Jacqueline Parker? J.P. Photography? I have a print of yours hanging in my husband's office!"

"Nice to meet you. I'm flattered you know about my work. Which print do you own?" I asked.

"It's one of a place we love, Door County. The cliffs in Peninsula Park, I believe."

"One of my favorites too."

"My husband, Senator Bennett, is in a meet and greet mode. I'm not as outgoing and good at small talk as he is."

Hannah offered to show Betsy where the powder room was. "And you're welcome to check out the antiques in the rooms that are open up here, too."

Betsy and I followed Hannah. "I admit I'd get turned around up here too," I told Betsy, noticing she still seemed anxious. Or maybe that was just her regular demeanor. Sounds of music and party chatter rose from the first floor as we passed the master staircase landing.

"Here you go, the lady's room."

It was locked, so we waited with Betsy. Eventually, Kim Walters opened the door.

"Well, look at you all looking so pretty. Mrs. Bennett, I believe," Kim said, extending her hand. "I'm Kim Walters, wife of our local newspaper owner. It's an honor to have you and the Senator here tonight. I must let Stuart know. Perhaps you'll speak to him?"

I was stunned that for once, it wasn't all about her. She was promoting her husband Stu this time and doing a good job of it.

But then the other shoe dropped when she said, "Perhaps you and your husband didn't realize that we are going to experience impressive growth when our new resort and condominium development is completed." She reached by her side, seeming to be looking for her purse. "I'm sorry. I seem to have misplaced my evening bag. I'll catch you later with my card on the chance that you and your husband decide to purchase one of the units. They'll be quite stunning."

Betsy wasn't sure what to make of Kim, but

graciously said, "Thank you." She quickly made her way into the bathroom, locking the door behind her.

I caught myself trying to see if there were champagne spills on Kim's dress as she stepped up to a hall mirror. Was she the lady in red who had gotten so upset with the waiter?

Hannah tapped my arm, indicating we should slip away to her office while Kim was distracted admiring herself in the mirror. I noticed Kim's eyes weren't on her image in the mirror, but on my reflection. "Oh Jackie, could I talk to you for a minute please?"

"Hannah, you get what you need. I'll wait for you here. Yes, Kim, what is it?"

Much to my chagrin, Kim spun toward me and started badmouthing Luella Hagge again.

"That woman makes me so angry. I keep telling everyone that the resort is coming soon. It'll be magnificent. I keep passing out my business cards like I just did to the Senator's wife. Staying positive and promoting what's coming." Kim took a breath, then, in a less sarcastic tone, said, "My reputation will be ruined. My good name crushed. Did you know that Luella Hagge has been the main reason this project is stalled yet again?"

I started to say something to cut off this conversation, but Kim interrupted me. "She is doing some crooked things with the land deal. Just because she runs Building and Zoning doesn't mean she can treat others like she does. She'll get hers."

All the while she's ranting, I sense she's been looking over my shoulder, not at me. I turned to see what she could be looking at, but there was nothing of note in the hall behind me.

Suddenly she switched gears. "I need to calm down. That's why I came up here. Sorry if I cornered you. I just feel a special bond with you." She stepped to the bannister on the landing, leaning over to peer down. "Oh exciting. They're getting ready for the raffle drawing and silent auction results."

And then, in an instant, everything went black.

The music stopped.

The party chatter stopped.

Low murmurings started.

Then a loud shout. "Everyone chill! Stay where you are. This is Scott Drake, I'm going down to the basement to check the breaker box. We probably just overloaded some circuits. Meanwhile use those cell phone flashlights."

A thump bump thump sounded in the darkness, followed by a scream.

CHAPTER FOUR

We were caught in a dark gloom. No moonlight broke through to light our way up here. But down below the glow from cell phones on the first floor showed a puddle of red at the bottom of the stairs.

"Step back, I'm a doctor. Let me through."

Through the parting crowd I made out Kim Walters. She moaned as the dark-haired figure of a doctor bent over her. With assistance, a disheveled Kim sat up. Her crown braid cocked, tilting to one side. Her feet were bare, her red high heels having slipped off in the tumbling fall.

The lights popped back on just as Betsy Bennett exited the bathroom and appeared behind me.

"Is she all right?" she asked.

Hannah hurried over to Betsy and me. "Are you both okay?"

"We are but look down there."

"Kim! Oh no!" Hannah said. "Did someone bump into her?"

"Wasn't me. I was in the powder room with my skirt up." Betsy giggled.

On my way down the staircase, I picked up Kim's shoes. The doctor had Kim standing now. I saw she was embarrassed by all the attention. Or was she enjoying it?

"I'm fine," she said, trying to assure everyone. Kim adjusted her crown, but it quickly settled back to the tilted angle. She didn't give up though and walked while casually holding one hand against the side of her head to support the hairdo. Like she thought none of us would notice.

"I'm taking you into my office for x-rays," the doctor said

"Nonsense, I told you I'm fine," Kim snapped. "Please step back and let me pull myself together here." She smiled awkwardly. "Let's all head over to the raffle table for the drawing!"

That got most of the gathered gawkers moving.

"Sorry Jackie, but I need to go help," Hannah said as she hustled off in the direction of the solarium.

I dangled Kim's shoes from my fingertips. She didn't

look too steady, but at least she didn't have anyone staring at her now. The doctor, a tall young woman with a pleasing face, kind eyes, and a short dark bob of hair still supported Kim, observing and trying to read Kim's signals.

"Are you certain about this?"

Kim took a deep breath. "Maybe I'll just sit on that bench and get my bearings for a minute."

"You'll be achy in the morning, but some ibuprofen should help with that," the doctor said.

"Yes, thank you, I'm okay. Just need to find my shoes and my evening bag."

I dangled the shoes in front of her. "I believe these are yours?"

Kim laughed, then grabbed her stomach. "Oops. No hard laughing for a while. Yes, those are mine. Did you see my bag too?"

"Nope I didn't. Remember you didn't have it to give Betsy your business card?"

Kim's face scrunched up in a puzzled expression. "That's right."

Betsy Bennett stood on a step above us. "Which rooms were you in?"

Kim hesitated. "The powder room and maybe one of the bedrooms. I was looking at the antiques displayed there. I'm not sure which one though."

Betsy quickly said, "I'll search for it." But then she looked across the group toward the front door. "Oh wait, my husband appears to want to leave."

I quickly stepped in and said, "Don't worry, I'll go look for her purse, Betsy. Kim, you stay right here on this bench. I'll go get your evening bag."

The doctor remained near her. "Please don't try to stay long. You really should get home."

"Kim, how are you?" Alan Morris hurried over. "I heard about your awful fall."

"Is this your husband, Kim?" the doctor asked.

"What? No!"

Alan said, "I'm a business associate of Kim's. I hurried over as soon as someone said a lady in a red dress had fallen down the staircase. I was in the kitchen area when the lights went out."

The first room I searched was the powder room, which turned out to be a complete bathroom. A claw-foot tub sat under a window. There was another door to the room, so it was probably part of a bedroom suite too. No purse in here.

I appeared back at the top of the stairs and called down to Kim. "No bag in here, but I'll keep looking for it."

"I'm leaving now, I'd be happy to take you home,"

Alan said. "Stuart was getting set up to take photos at the silent auction and raffle tables."

"Good idea, Kim," I said. "I would hate to drag Stu away from the work he loves."

"Yes, Alan, I'll accept your offer," Kim said. "Jackie, please let Stuart know I'm going home and give him my bag when you find it. Thank you so much."

I returned to my search, by looking in the rooms open to the public. I discovered Hannah's office, and three bedrooms set up for guests to tour. Lamps turned on. Beds made up. But no red purse.

I was about ready to give up. But then I remembered that door in the guest bathroom. I went back and tried it. The room I entered was dark, but with a flick of the switch the lights came on to reveal a bedroom all done up in pink. A window seat across the space caught my eye. I'd always loved those. Through the window I saw the full moon. That meant I must be toward the back of the house.

Like Hannah said, the period pieces left in these rooms were amazing. Across the pink bedroom I saw light coming in under another door. I was getting a little confused. That must be one of the rooms open to the public, and I'd already checked those for Kim's purse.

I turned out the bedroom lights and stepped back into the bathroom. As I closed the door between the two rooms, I heard a loud sound. I looked back into the darkness of the pink bedroom and walked toward the door across the room. The door to a room with a light on.

Behind this door I made a discovery. Not Kim's evening bag, but a body.

CHAPTER FIVE

Within ten minutes, Chief of Police Jeff Mathis stood next to me. "It's nice to see you again Jackie, just not under these circumstances. The first time we met was next to a body, and here we are again."

"Yes, it was. I was thinking the same thing when I placed the 911 call." I noted Jeff still wore his graying hair slightly longer than regulation. It suited him. Instead of his uniform, he wore jeans and a blue and white checked shirt rolled at the cuffs.

The first body he referred to was Paul Griffin, Eleanor Harmony's fiancé. Wanda and I found him in a wrecked car on the side of Harmony Hill. That time I'd taken crime scene photos out of instinct. This time that task was being handled by the police, because now the death was obviously a murder, based on the bloody wound on the back of the victim's head.

Officer Patrick Murphy, known as Murph, appeared in the doorway of the room where we stood. "I stopped any more people from leaving and the County Sheriff is sending help, Chief."

"Thanks, Murph. Jackie, I appreciate you preventing anyone from coming up here to disturb the scene."

"I did ask Dr. Trueblood to make sure Luella Hagge wasn't still alive. My skills at determining death are not up to hers."

"Please call me Dawn," the doctor said. "It appears the cause of death was a blow to the back of her head, but an autopsy will verify that. My guess is the weapon is lying next to her. Time of death? Probably within fifteen minutes of Jackie finding the victim."

Luella Hagge's body lay face down on the floor. Her red gown swirled across the intricate patterns of the Oriental rug she fell on. The room was surprisingly undisturbed, except for a large heavy vase resting on its side next to her.

"It would seem so." Jeff directed another officer to bag the vase. "Have the remaining guests been gathered together?"

"Yes sir," Murph said. "This will be a long night. Are you going to question everyone that was here?"

A woman entered the room, her identification badge on a lanyard around her neck. "Hey Jeff. Good to see you. What have we got here?"

"Lou…this is a nice surprise. Glad to be working with you again. The last time was that runaway case, right? Dr. Trueblood and Jackie Parker, meet Detective Louise Taylor. She's with the County Sheriff's department. We lean on them to help with investigations on certain cases."

Detective Taylor was a medium height, middle-aged woman who looked more like a librarian, with horn-rimmed glasses and a bun at the nape of her neck, than a detective.

With the discovery of Luella's body, the festive quality of the night shifted quickly into something darker. Someone had been murdered up here, while the party was going on downstairs. A heaviness descended over Harmony House.

When I entered the plant-filled solarium where most of the people were gathered, all eyes turned toward me. They learned I discovered the body but didn't quite know what to make of it. This had been a long evening, and I was happy to see Aunt Ruth saving a place for me to sit. It was looking to be even longer as I took in the size of the group waiting to be interviewed. Not only party guests, but the caterer Darlene, waiters, and the Murphy's. It was their son Officer Patrick Murphy who was here working the case. We nodded at each other across the room. I could imagine they just wanted out of here. But I understood that any of these people might hold a clue to lead the police to the murderer. On a more disturbing note, any of them could be the murderer.

Chief Jeff Mathis and Detective Louise Taylor introduced themselves to those assembled. They explained who the victim was and the basic crime scene.

"If any of you here has specific information that you feel would be relevant to our investigation, please raise your hand," Detective Taylor said.

No one raised their hand.

Jeff spoke. "We will be interviewing each of you individually. We will try to get through these opening questions quickly as I realize the hour is late. I recognize many of you so remember, I know where to find you."

His attempt at lightening the mood brought out a hesitant laugh from a few of those assembled.

"Many of you will be sent home and contacted later if we have more questions as we get further into the investigative process. My staff are still working the crime scene."

Jeff quickly allowed many of the potential witnesses to leave after confirming they would be available for further questioning.

The solarium began emptying. My dear Aunt Ruth had been offered numerous rides home but stayed to wait for my questioning to be over.

"This is quite a different, what do the kids call it? A different vibe then when we held our garden club meetings in this room," she said.

"I'll bet it is. I hope we get called up soon. I'm eager to get back to that little balcony on the studio and have a relaxing glass of wine with you." I had planned to talk to Ruth about my ideas for the photography studio tonight, but it looked like that would have to wait until tomorrow.

The state senator Robert Bennett and his wife Betsy were long gone. They left right after Scott got the lights turned back on. I reminded myself to tell Jeff that Betsy had been upstairs using the powder room when the lights went out. Dr. Trueblood placed the time of death within fifteen minutes from when I called her up to the room. So, Luella could have been struck on the back of her head before the lights went out. I'd have to ask Scott if he remembered the time he turned them back on, and for how long they had been out.

Stuart Walters sat quietly in the corner. He seemed

overwhelmed by it all. His wife Kim had accepted Alan Morris's offer to take her home, so he was alone here.

The caterer was still here. Some of her staff had been sent home earlier, as most of the hors d'oeuvre and champagne serving was wrapped up before the raffle drawing. I'd seen them leaving by the back door when I came in to meet Hannah earlier. It appeared there were about five catering staff still here. Most had taken off their black ties and loosened their collars. A couple of them had their jackets on, ready to leave. Darlene tried to get permission from Jeff to work in the kitchen for a head start on packing up.

The Murphy's looked to do the same. They'd been gracious enough to brew fresh coffee for anyone still waiting.

Scott Drake was concerned about the electrical issues that apparently blew the main breaker and had been released to further check on the situation.

Hannah, who had been near the scene of the crime, waited to be questioned more extensively. She busied herself cleaning up the raffle and silent auction tables.

My turn came to be interviewed.

Detective Taylor seemed to have an easy relationship with Jeff. I wondered how long they had known each other. Her black jacket lay on the chair next to her now. The librarian appearance disappeared as soon as I saw the muscular definition in her upper arms and shoulders. I could see she kept herself in good shape.

"Jackie, I understand you found Ms. Hagge's body, is that correct?" The detective asked me.

"Yes. I was looking for Kim Walters' evening bag which she left in one of the second-floor rooms."

Detective Taylor referred to her notes. "She was the woman who fell down the staircase just after the lights went out, is that correct?"

"Yes, that was Kim."

Jeff spoke up, telling the detective, "She left to go home and lie down before the victim was discovered. We'll be interviewing her tomorrow. But her husband Stuart is still here. He's with the local newspaper."

The detective nodded. She was all business now. "Go on Ms. Parker, tell me about the time before the lights went out?"

"Hannah Sutton and I, she's the antique dealer who is working with the Historical Society to catalog and appraise the various items in this home, had come down from the attic to the second floor with the intent of her showing me some additional garments."

"Wait, let me get this clear. You were on the second floor, presumably when the murder occurred?"

I shrugged. "Based on Dr. Trueblood's time of death, I suppose I could have been."

"You used the words looking at garments. Why?"

I explained about the wardrobe of clothes from my mother's dress shop being in the attic. "We entered the attic by the back stairway from the kitchen and then, instead of going back down to the first floor, we got off on the second floor and there stood Betsy Bennett. She and Hannah knew each other. We exchanged a few words about antiques."

"Mrs. Bennett was in the second-floor hallway. Did she say why?"

I had to think. It was odd how she was just standing there in the hall. "I'm not sure to be honest. She said she got turned around. Oh, now I remember, she said she was looking for the powder room. There was only one restroom in use on the main floor you understand."

Detective Taylor nodded. "I see, thank you. Did you hear or see anything else unusual? Chief Mathis mentioned you are a very observant person, probably because of your career as a photographer."

"Kim Walters was there too. She came out of the powder room as Betsy entered it," I said, then stopped. Should I tell them about Kim going on and on about Luella Hagge? To me it felt like the drama Kim displays often. Or did it mean something more? Jeff was letting the detective run this show. He seemed comfortable doing that. It would have felt easier talking to him because he knew Kim. But at least he's here to listen and help assess the information.

"Did she at any time mention Ms. Hagge?"

"She did seem upset about Luella in a professional capacity. She was grumbling about some delays on the resort development project. That it was getting bogged down waiting for approval from the Building and Zoning board."

"I see." The detective noted what I said in her notebook, then pen to mouth, she paused before asking the next question. "What caused Kim to fall down the staircase?"

"I'm not sure. She looked down over the railing saying that the raffle drawing would begin soon. Then the power shut off. Scott shouted for everyone to stay where they were. Next thing I heard was her falling, or rather I should say I heard someone falling. She might have tripped on her gown or took a step in the dark and missed the staircase. Then the lights came on and everyone's attention focused on Kim lying on the floor."

"Tell me Jackie, why did you go to the room where you found the victim?" Detective Taylor's demeanor seemed to change. More intense, focused.

"Kim misplaced her evening bag. I told her I'd check around upstairs. I'd already looked in the powder room. Kim sat at the bottom of the staircase waiting for me to find her purse. When the doctor encouraged her to leave, I agreed to continue looking for it and give it to her husband Stuart. Then an associate offered to take her home, and she seemed relieved to leave. So, I went back to searching the rooms open to the public."

"It's my understanding that the room the victim was found in was not open to the public Ms. Parker. Is that correct?"

"Yes, it is."

"Why did you choose that room to look in, Ms. Parker? How did you end up at the scene of the crime?"

CHAPTER SIX

Quiet Sunday morning in a small town. My hands clasped a mug filled with hot coffee. After a restless night on my bed, aka the couch, I'd finally decided to get up. I threw on my robe and sat out on the little balcony overlooking Main Street.

It was so late when we got home last night that wine was the last thing on my mind. But it might have helped me sleep. The events of the evening kept popping up. Was there something I'd forgotten during the interview? Any more evidence I could provide to help them solve the murder?

Ruth appeared, her own coffee cup in hand.

"Sorry if I woke you Aunt Ruth."

"You didn't. This one did. I took her for her morning walk in the back. I've been up for a while."

Libby licked my bare ankles. I picked her up and held her on my lap. She turned once in a circle then curled herself up in a ball.

"Long night for us kiddo," Ruth said, easing herself into the other chair on the balcony. "Thanks for making our morning coffee. So, now for the big question, who do you think killed Luella?"

"Frankly I'm trying to remain detached from what happened. I can't get caught up in this. I have something big on my mind."

"Aren't you curious? I am."

"Sure, I'm curious, you know me. But I'm trying to curb my curiosity this time. The thing I have on my mind right now involves you."

Ruth's eyes narrowed. "Me?"

"Ever since I met your friends at Shady Pines and saw what a beautiful place it was, I knew I wouldn't feel bad about kicking you out of this apartment. After all, I'm in my sixties, and sleeping on your couch is not what it used be when I was in my youth." I casually took a sip of coffee as if I had not dropped a bombshell in her lap.

Aunt Ruth sat staring at me. Her mouth gaped open. Her coffee cup suspended midair. Birds flitted and chirped. Church bells tolled. Motorboats pulled out of the small marina. A dog barked nearby.

Ruth slowly set her cup down. "You're kicking me out of my own place? Excuse me, but that doesn't make any sense."

"I'm hoping it'll be my place, because I'd like to make you a serious offer on this building. And that would include buying the business of Parker Photography."

"You know it's yours in my will, don't you?"

"I didn't, but thank you for that. The point though is that I like what's happening here in Harmony and I think this would be a good business move on my part."

"To take over this business? What on earth for? It's hardly a thriving photography studio."

"I realize that. But I have a vision for it. And I certainly want it to stay in our family."

"Jacqueline Parker. You are a famous photographer. You travel the world taking only the jobs you choose. You don't need a business here in Harmony."

I put on a pouting face. "So, you don't want to see me here more often?"

"Don't you do that to me. I will not accept a charity offer from my niece. I'm fine right here above the studio."

"I know you are. But don't you see? I want something more permanent. An actual place where people know me. And a gallery for my work plus that of other photographers. Now I'm isolated. My work is in someone else's gallery…or a big ad campaign…or a magazine spread…or a coffee-table book. But those aren't places that people can step into. I want somewhere to hang my own work and that of my fellow artists. And I'm totally serious about the couch. I'm grateful knowing it's always here for me to use, but I want to keep clothes here, my own brand of shampoo and conditioner, spices I use to cook with. I want my own place here in Harmony, knowing I can spend more than a couple of days and not be in your way."

"You're never in my way, Jackie. You are really serious about this aren't you?"

I felt my own plan, vision, whatever I called it, becoming more concrete in my mind. I'd finally spoken the words out loud, and I liked the sound of them. "Yes I am. I'm willing to make you a fair offer."

Ruth slumped back in her chair. Confused. Uncertain.

"You don't have to answer me right now. But please think about it. I'm excited at the possibility of working here again. And living here, at least part time. Who knows, it might turn into more time than I expect. I don't want to retire and having a business like this seems a perfect fit."

She held up her hand to halt my words. Had I said something wrong? Was I missing something? "I can answer you now, Jackie. Yes, yes, yes...ten thousand times yes."

We both leaped up and reached our arms out for hugs.

"Whoa up there. Careful now that you two don't fall off that old balcony." Someone shouted up from the sidewalk below us. It was Stuart Walters. His charmingly full cheeks rose in a big smile. "What are you two all wound up about? Something you want to share with me? Maybe a news scoop."

"All in good time, Stu," Aunt Ruth called down. "How's Kim doing after that awful fall last night?"

"She's planning on resting today. In fact, she's still asleep. Pretty achy I suppose," Stu said. "Say, did they figure out who killed Luella Hagge?"

Stu looked comical as he bent his head back and shaded his eyes from the morning sun, waiting for his answer.

"We don't know," Ruth told him.

"Well let me know if you hear anything. I'm going to the office today. Lots of stuff to write up. Got some good photographs of last night's events. And I want to do some research on Luella Hagge. I believe she once worked for the village in some capacity. Do you remember that, Ruth?"

"Can't say I do," Ruth answered. "Patti at the village hall might know. She's been there quite awhile."

"Good idea. But she won't be in until tomorrow. Do you have her phone number?"

"I can get it from my assistant, Mandy. Patti is her mother-in-law. I'll call you with it in a few minutes."

And with that Stuart Walters set off for his office just two short blocks further down on Main Street.

"Now back to our conversation," Ruth said. "I can't believe you want Parker Photography. I would feel funny selling it though. It's as much yours as it is mine."

"It's only fair. When you buy that little cottage at Shady Pines, you can leave it to me in your will. I might just end up living there one day."

Ruth gasped. "Oh my gosh…yes. That's fair."

"Absolutely fair." I was so happy! This had worked out perfectly. Ruth could feel it was not a charity buy, but an exchange of sorts.

"This is the most amazing day. I can't wait to tell the girls! But first let me get hold of Mandy for Patti's phone number." She started walking inside, but suddenly spun around. "I have one request regarding you taking over the business. You must let Mandy stay on. At least let her prove herself to you. She's been a wonderful help for me. And she's eager to learn more about the business."

I nodded, trying to look thoughtful. I ran my hand over Libby's back. "Before I commit to that, I have one for you. That Libby remain as Parker Photography's mascot."

Libby had been Mandy's dog, but when her new husband developed allergies to her, Ruth had agreed to keep her at the studio temporarily.

Libby looked up at me with a soft tilt of her head. "Yes girl. You can be our guard and greeter dog. Deal?" I held my hand out for a paw shake which I got.

"I will if you promise to let me borrow her occasionally, like when you have to travel. Deal?" Ruth said.

"Deal!"

And so, it was settled. That was easier than I thought it would be. I expected all sorts of arguments from Ruth. She was fine right here. She didn't need my money. She could sell the business on her own. But nope, she agreed to my idea. This was going to happen. I'm going to own a business in Harmony! Now to get Scott Drake here to start putting together ideas for remodeling the place.

Again, someone shouted up to us, "Good morning."

It was Mandy letting herself into the studio. "I want to hear how the party went last night."

"Come on up," Ruth said, before turning to me. "Can I let her in on our plans?"

"Absolutely. I hope she'll agree to stay. We made her a bargaining chip without her even knowing. Fingers crossed she'll want to stay."

We presented our plans for the studio, which included Mandy working here.

"That's amazing news. I'm so happy for you, Ruth and for you, Jackie. This sounds perfect. And I'd be honored to work with you, Jackie. But what about Libby? Will you take her to Shady Pines with you, Ruth?"

"No. I love her but waking up early every morning to a cold nose nudging me because she needs to go out is not my thing. Libby is going to become the mascot for the gallery, or studio, or shop, or whatever it will be called."

"And guard dog. Don't forget guard dog," I said. "Though not like that one at Cutter's. The salvage yard had a huge vicious Doberman Pinscher who raised a ruckus and lunged again and again at his fence. More gentile…" We all laughed at the image of sweet gentle Libby doing anything at all like Spike. I remembered my visit to that salvage yard when I tried to figure out what really happened on the Saturday night before Eleanor

Harmony's wedding. An interesting place to say the least.

"First order of business will be to get your father-in-law over here to give us some remodeling ideas. And get the sales documents drawn up. I'm hoping we can wrap a lot of this up before I leave."

Mandy said, "Matt and his dad went fishing this morning. But when they get back, I'll talk to him. This is so exciting!"

"Hello up there."

The three of us looked across Main Street where Hannah Sutton stood outside her antique store. If I'm spending more time here, I'm going to have to get used to the fact that the people walking by know me, unlike Chicago where they stare straight ahead or at their phones as they push their way along the sidewalks.

"Good morning, Hannah," Ruth called out. "Opening up early today?"

"Mark's opening up later. I just needed to pick up some things before I head up to Harmony House. Jackie, I hoped you'd join me. I meant to talk to you more about the treasure trove of decades of fashion stored there. I have some ideas for preserving them and displaying them I wanted to share with you. Plus, if you'll agree I'd like to lean on your artistic eye and photographic abilities."

"You're a sweet talker Hannah," I said. "I would love to meet you up there. Are the police opening up the house for you?"

"Parts of it are still sealed off, but we should be able to access the attic and our Historical Society offices."

"Can I bring along my new little buddy?" I lifted Libby's paws up against the railing.

Hannah laughed. "Of course. I'm leaving now and I see you're still in your robe and enjoying your morning coffee. But can you join me up there shortly?"

CHAPTER SEVEN

Detective Taylor was coming down the big staircase and had stopped to speak with an officer waiting at the bottom.

"Morning Detective," I said as I entered.

"Good morning Ms. Parker. You're just the person I wanted to see. Hannah is here and has walked me through what she remembers happening last night. She did a reenactment of where you two were before and after the lights went out. There was a period you were separated, I'd like to understand where you were during that time."

Was she implying I did something wrong? Or suspected that Hannah or I were somehow involved with Luella's murder?

My internal questions must have shown on my face,

because Detective Taylor quickly said, “Please don’t think I’m suggesting you need to have an alibi for your time, but we just want a broader sense of where everyone was during the time period of the murder. There were many people here when it occurred, and we need to weave all the different details together to get a clearer picture to discover discrepancies or holes.”

Whew, I thought. Realizing how I felt, I knew I’d make a bad criminal if I was actually guilty of something. “Sure, I’d be happy to, Detective. Just let me find Hannah first and let her know I’ll be with you for a few minutes.”

With a humorless smile, Detective Taylor said, “Now don’t go comparing stories though.”

I found Hannah gathering up the remnants of the auction and raffle activities. A young man was helping her put the furniture back in order. Rolling the large potted plants back to where they’d been. Moving the beautiful wicker furniture back into position. The solarium, with the morning sun spilling in through the glass walls and roof, looked so different from last night. Hard to believe what had transpired here and on what should have been such a joyous occasion of celebrating this mansion’s transformation.

“It’ll take a while to distribute the prizes and make sure everything is accounted for. Can you hang on a moment?" Hannah said, looking stressed. Were we both under suspicion? Had the detective just said those words to calm me?

"Hannah, I just wanted to let you know that Detective Taylor wants to talk to me now. I heard you talked with her about last night."

Hannah pulled me to a quiet corner. "I did. It felt strange. It's hard remembering everything so exactly. Be careful what you say. I told the truth as I remembered it, but I was so nervous. I'm sure she's going to compare what we each say happened."

"She seems really interested in the time we weren't together. You left with Stuart to take photographs. I just wandered around alone. I didn't talk to anyone. I don't have an alibi."

"Jackie don't be silly. You don't need an alibi. Besides, I'm sure someone saw you. You didn't go upstairs, did you?"

"No, I went outside. So, there was hardly anyone else out there. How can I prove that's what I did?"

Someone coughed behind us, and we both jumped. "Excuse me Ms. Parker, but are you ready to go through last night with me? Let's start with the time period when you and Hannah were separated. She went with..." Detective Taylor looked at her notes, flipping back a couple of pages. "She left with Stuart Walters, which he has already confirmed, to take some photographs. Please come with me, Ms. Parker."

I gave a little wave to Hannah and walked off with the detective.

"Hannah and I were going up to the attic because she was going to show me something she'd found. But Stu, Stuart Walters, snagged Hannah for some photographs for his paper, the Harmony Hills Happenings. Oh, wait you know that already."

"Yes, I do."

Don't let your nerves get to you, I told myself. Having my new little Libby with me made me feel better, too. I was glad I brought her along. "While they were doing their thing, I decided to check out the raffle tables and the band in the solarium. The room had quite a few people in it, but I didn't recognize any of them, so I stepped outside."

"Take me there now please," the detective said.

We stepped out on to the paver patio edged with flower beds. The place looked so different in the light of day. "I remember that the moon was full, and the surrounding grounds were lit up. The luminaria created an appealing, welcoming mood. I looked back up at the house with its vine-covered walls, just enjoying the evening. I remembered Eleanor showing us her father's office last time I was here, and I noted lights were on in there and some people were moving about."

"Did you recognize them?" the detective asked.

"No. Though one silhouette reminded me of Alan Morris, because he moves with a slight limp. Then I went back inside after just a few minutes."

"Anything else you noted when you were outside?"

"Nothing I can think of. The music was good! But I guess that's not a clue."

Stop acting so nervous Jackie, I told myself again. You have nothing to hide. "I did note that someone was smoking a cigar further out from the house. Couples were strolling across the lawns. I just remember feeling so happy that this beautiful place would be taken care of. I saw lights on in the upstairs windows. The music being played was great. Wait, I said that already. I do remember the time! The band announced that the raffle drawing would happen in thirty minutes. So, thirty minutes earlier than that was to happen was when I was out here."

"Okay, those are good details. Now take me inside. You say Hannah was here in the solarium?"

"No. I didn't say that. I met her in the kitchen. I walked to the side door and waited for her in there. She was going to show me the back staircase that would take us up to the third-floor attic."

"Please be sure to keep in mind any conversations you overheard, or since you're a photographer, any images you saw. Any gesturing or body language that seemed out of place. Chief Jeff told me your instincts and curiosity were instrumental in solving a case here in Harmony just a short time ago."

Was she trying to make me relaxed and say something I didn't mean to? "He did? Hmm...let's say my curiosity pushes me a little. Hard for me to ignore it sometimes."

"Please continue to keep your awareness up while you're in town. I've found that at times things will be said in front of someone who is not familiar, not local. People let their guard down thinking their stories won't be repeated because you're a stranger here."

A stranger here? Is that how people see me? I grew up in Harmony. I have old friends here. But what she said is true. So many new people, new generations. But it is still my hometown. Am I wrong in thinking I can just swoop in and take over the family business? Focus Jackie. Get back to this moment. "Sure. Okay. I'm planning on staying a few days."

"Great. Please don't leave until we've cleared you. Now, back to our tour. You said you went through the kitchen."

I tried to pull my memories from last night into a

sharper focus. I told the detective how Hannah and I wove through the busyness of the people working in the kitchen. Grace and Dermot Murphy, proprietors of Murphy's, a local coffee shop and bakery, were arranging dessert trays. We greeted each other, spoke pleasantries, and I snagged a cup of coffee from them. I'd had enough champagne and the evening air on the patio had been just a touch chilly.

"Sounds like you know quite a few people in town," the detective said. "Anything else you'd like to remark on?"

Wait, there was something that happened here. I tried to reverse the scene. What was it? The sound of dishes banging. Food odors as piping hot hors d'oeuvres came out of the oven. The place was busy. Snippets of conversations. Then I remembered the spilled champagne.

"A waiter came running in saying a woman had gotten champagne spilled on her dress. Darlene said to give the woman her business card so they could clean the dress. My back was to them. I don't know which waiter it was."

Even as we were speaking, the caterer Darlene entered the room through the back door. Her laughing and talking interrupted my train of thought. "Detective, I rounded up these two for you," she said.

"Thanks, can you give me a few minutes while I finish up with Ms. Parker?"

"Sure, we'll wait outside."

"You seemed to remember something more, Ms. Parker?"

I laughed awkwardly. "As I age, I have to hang on tight to thoughts or they are simply gone! I guess maybe it was nothing. I did see her in the kitchen, she's the caterer, right?"

"Yes. And those two are servers who had left earlier in the evening. Just wanted to make sure to talk to them. Wait staff move around and hear and see things at parties. I'll question the caterer about the incident you mentioned."

I turned back to determine if I recognized the two waiters, but they had already left the kitchen. Detective Taylor watched me as she held the door open to the back staircase. I took a deep breath and entered the narrow passage.

The next minutes were spent in me trying to recall and then tell the detective things I remembered about last night. Who Hannah and I saw on the second floor. Our interactions with Betsy Bennett and Kim Walters. She made notes and even flipped to previous pages once or twice. I was about finished when she said, "I'm sorry if I've made you nervous. I didn't mean for this to feel like an inquisition. Is there something you're not telling me?" She looked at me expectantly. We stood near the top of the main staircase.

"Ah no. I don't believe so. We froze in place when the lights went out like I said. And the sense of someone running past us, stopping, continuing on, and then Kim falling."

"Running? I thought you said the person was hurrying."

"Yes, I mean hurrying. Footsteps walking fast. Not running full steam ahead."

"I see. You mentioned that last night. But when I interviewed you later, you said Kim might have tripped, or took a misstep on the stairs. Hmm…"

She's right. There was that moment I thought I heard footsteps. In the light of day, I'm not so sure. I tried explaining, but Detective Taylor quickly said, "You have my card, if you think of something else, please don't hesitate to call."

At that moment Scott came up the staircase, and the detective walked up to him. I heard them discussing the situation with the electrical panel in the basement.

"Excuse me, are we done?" I asked.

Detective Taylor looked at me and nodded, before turning back to Scott. But then she stopped and looked toward me again.

"Wait a second, Ms. Parker. You didn't mention that Kim left with Alan Morris. Did you see that?"

"I didn't think to mention it. Have you talked to her?"

"I'm still waiting to interview her. Her husband said she was resting today. Oh, and we found her purse. It had slipped behind a piece of furniture in the room where Luella was murdered." Detective Taylor snapped her notebook shut and said, "Thought you might like to know that."

Whoa! That's surprising news. I'd never considered asking if the purse was found. Are they leaning toward Kim as the suspect and thought she fled the scene? Or was she trying to catch me saying something wrong?

I used the powder room, and since the pink bedroom wasn't blocked off with crime scene tape, I looked inside. I felt a small draft. The window appeared to be cracked open. I walked over to close it and saw I was right above that beautiful trellis I noticed last night. Hmm, is that a flowering vine? Looks like a small white bud down below. What a view from up here. I closed the window. I should let Hannah know as it wouldn't do to have antiques exposed to the damp night air.

Libby was getting a little fidgety. Oh gosh, she might need to go to the bathroom. I'd lost track of time. I'll have to make sure I learn her signals.

Leaving through the solarium doors, I walked Libby

around the side of the house. No baggie, oops…I'll have to travel with her more prepared next time!

The fresh mulch spread in the beds here smelled so good. I waited for Libby to do her business as my eyes took in my surroundings in the daytime. This was the side of the house where I found the open window a few moments ago. I stood at the base of the sturdy-looking trellis with a hardy vine wrapping its way upward. I'll bet this looks gorgeous when fully leafed out in summer.

"Libby, come on girl. Don't get tangled up in those vines." She seemed intent on reaching something caught at the roots of the vine. Five small orange raffle ticket stubs stapled together and a paper cocktail napkin. I glanced at the number sequence, my birthday. These could have been my lucky numbers. But not to be…hope someone got lucky with the win.

I dropped the tickets along with the paper napkin in the trash on my way through the house. Wait…maybe someone will be looking for these? Did they have to keep the stub to confirm? I pulled the tickets back out and tucked them in my pocket.

CHAPTER EIGHT

In the late afternoon, Ruth and I took a nice walk along the river ending up at the Harmony Diner for dinner, or as they call it in this part of the world, supper. We ordered the chicken and dumplings. Ruth told me about her visit with her friends at Shady Pines earlier today.

"I hope you don't mind me jumping the gun a little. If I keep spreading the word around, you won't be able to back out on me."

"Aunt Ruth, I have absolutely no intention of backing out. In fact, I've even let some other photographer friends know I will be opening a gallery here where they can exhibit. I'll say the same thing to you. You can't back out either! What do the gals think about it?"

"They are excited for me. They know that it's a good time in my life to slow down."

"And get away from having to climb those stairs to the apartment above the studio," I added.

"Right. Only there's one not so good thing. Do you remember that Duke who passed away? His little cottage has been up for sale for quite a while, so I figured it would be perfect for me. But it's under a sales contract," Ruth said with a huge sigh. "I don't know when another one will open up."

I didn't know she'd planned to visit them today or I would have told her. I quickly took her hands in mine across the table. "Aunt Ruth, it's under contract for you! I talked with Kim about it weeks ago when I began making my decision to offer to buy your business. I didn't want it to be sold. I'm so sorry. I was planning to tell you last night, but well, you understand, other things got in the way."

A relieved smile pulled at her lips. "I can't believe you did that! You are just the dearest sweetest niece. Thank you for securing it for me. Now I can do a happy dance for sure."

We enjoyed our supper and toasted to the months ahead and the happy changes to come.

On our walk back home, I noticed Sutton Antiques across the street from our studio, soon to be my studio. I was reminded about it being my mother's dress shop long ago. "Aunt Ruth," I said. "I didn't get to tell you about why Hannah and I were even on the second floor of the mansion last night when Kim fell down the stairs."

"And Luella was murdered," Ruth added.

"Right. Hannah and I had just been up in the third-floor attic area. She was in the process of pulling out items, furniture, paintings, and stuff, including an extensive collection of clothing from decades ago. It's really quite something. When the dust settles around getting the mansion set up for tourists and as a museum, she's talking about us creating a book using these well-preserved garments. Like fashion through time in a small Wisconsin river town."

"I'd love to see those myself. The Harmonys, being a wealthy family, would go to the big cities to shop," Ruth said.

"They did. But they also purchased dresses at Mom's place. Hannah showed me the tags that read *Vogue on Main*."

"Yes. I remember your mother handling some custom lines. They used to do that, add labels for the dress shop it was going to. My goodness. What a find for Hannah. Was Jeff out at Harmony House today?"

"I didn't see him, but Detective Taylor found me. And she grilled me again."

"Do you think they have some ideas about who did it?"

"You mean besides me?"

Ruth paled and stared at me. "They suspect you? What on earth?"

"I might be overdramatizing it a bit. Maybe it's just her style, but I sure felt uncomfortable."

Ruth gave me a slap on my arm. "Don't do that to me! But seriously, who would murder someone like that? And why?"

We got in our pajamas and watched the ten o'clock local news out of Greensville. There was a segment on the murder of Luella Hagge. The reporter added details about Luella's time working in the Village of Harmony where she met her death. Then her return to law school and opening her own small firm in Greensville before beginning her career in public service as the head of Building and Zoning for the county. She reported that now Luella had been making a run for the office of District Attorney. They did a brief interview with her opponent in the DA race, Len Lampert.

Ruth burst out laughing as she listened to Len speak. "What a two-faced so and so. The guy's a liar, saying he's so sorry that his opponent lost her life. Yeah right, he is. I saw him taking down her yard signs today! He didn't even wait until the body was cold."

The segment ended with the reporter saying that since both the local and county law enforcement agencies are involved in the investigation, the case should be closed soon. In fact, they had a statement from the County Sheriff saying just that.

"When I visited the gals today, we hashed over some ideas we had about who might have done it. Did they give a time of death yet? None of us heard anything about that, but since you found the body and were right in the room with the police when they arrived, the gals suggested you might know."

I could picture them doing that. Dorothy, Eunice, and Betty liked to know what was going on in Harmony and the classic murder when the lights go out would be sure to pique their interest. "The medical examiner, our own local physician, Dr. Trueblood, put the time of death within a twenty-minute window," I said. "Did any of you see something at the party? Or overhear anything?"

"Chief Jeff talked briefly to all of us last night. None of us had anything of value to add. I stayed around to wait for you, and I shared anything I picked up in the waiting area with them."

"And what did you hear there?" I asked.

She shrugged "Nothing of particular interest. Everyone still there was shocked. But then murmurs about why, how, and who did it, began to make the rounds. I heard that when she was in private practice, she made a few enemies. And that she was being pretty nasty to that sweet sincere Len Lampert who just shared his shock and grief for the cameras."

"Was she from Harmony?"

"Good question. I'm not sure. Anyway, like I was saying, the gals remembered you being involved with the Paul Griffin case."

"Yes. Odd how that happened. How is Eleanor doing? I heard she's with Tom out at the house Scott remodeled."

"Yes, and I couldn't be happier for her. But you didn't say what you found out. Better yet, what you suspect. You were practically in the room with her and the murderer."

"I don't have a sense about anyone, except that detective. She's tenacious. Betsy, Senator Bennett's wife, was there and used the powder room. So, we chatted with her a little about antiques. Kim hovered around. Let's see. Hannah and me. There might have been a couple of other people checking out the open rooms, but I don't remember them. Then the announcement about the raffle drawings and final auction bids. The lights turned out, Kim fell down the stairs, and that's about it, until I went looking for her purse and found Luella."

"Why no blood-curdling scream from you when you discovered her body?"

"Well, in my work, I've seen dead bodies and I've seen panic. Remember I worked a few crime scenes early on to make ends meet. Anyway, I made a split-second decision that the entire house full of people didn't have to learn about Luella that very second."

After Ruth went to bed, I stepped out on the balcony. I loved that about this place. From here, I could see up and down Main Street and between buildings down to the river where it widened to form a small lake. The marina lights created a soft glow in the distance and in the clear night air I heard the muted clanging sounds from sailboats rocking gently in their docks. There were only a few sailboats in our marina. Most people used pontoons, speed boats, or fishing boats. The lake, as we called it, was just a generously sized part of the river formed by a dam downstream. The moon was partially obscured by a small thin strip of clouds. Across the street, several lights were on in Sutton Antiques. For both ambiance and security, I imagined.

Memories of me standing up here as a child waiting for Mom to finish up her day or watching stylish ladies enter the store to shop crossed my mind. Aunt Ruth lived here in this apartment as long as I remember. Dad told me she had a beau, and they'd planned to marry, but he drowned in a boating accident. She became something of a mother figure to me. She and Dad did what I loved…took pictures.

Aunt Ruth told me I was my mother's little mannequin. Looking back, I do remember when Mom got a new shipment of high-end children's clothing from one of her buying trips to New York were the times I got the most attention from her. Fashion was not my passion, but it was hers.

CHAPTER NINE

Early Monday morning I received a call from Stuart to stop in if I had a chance. He sounded troubled by something, so I hurried over as soon as I'd finished my morning coffee.

The office was a short walk away. I took the time to clear my head. On the phone call Stuart had told me Kim hadn't been interviewed. That she was still resting. I'm sure Jeff wouldn't put up with that story much longer, unless she really was in bad shape and under a doctor's supervision.

I found Stuart sitting behind his big desk. I didn't get the usual welcome and offer of coffee and a donut. In fact, the office had a palpable dullness to it.

"Thank you for coming so soon Jackie. I just can't get

this article about Saturday night completed. I want to turn back the clock."

"Stu let me get us some coffee at Murphy's. And a box of donuts like you always have here. I'll be right back."

"No. Don't leave. Please lock the door. I don't want us to be interrupted," he snapped.

Stuart Walters never snaps. I jumped to and locked the door.

"I've done the piece showcasing the Historical Society and the fundraiser. Put in a few photographs too. But I can't pull together the other event. The event that everyone will expect to be on the front page. I know I have to cover it, but my heart just isn't in. I mean my wife…"

He's obviously distraught. "Is Kim okay? Has she been examined by a doctor?"

"She looked so beautiful in that red dress, didn't she?"

"Yes, she looked lovely. Stu, can I help you with anything? Please don't be afraid to ask."

He seemed to pull himself together before saying, "Can you help me decide how much back story I should put in about Luella? I've pulled up so many things from her past."

"Sure Stuart. Can you show me some of the things

you've found? We'll get this done and then you can head home to Kim. The authorities will be wanting to talk to her."

"We realize that. We've been avoiding their calls."

I was pouring over Stuart's research when we heard a door close at the back of the offices, making us both jump. Things certainly were on edge here.

"Darling! What are you doing here?" Stuart exclaimed.

It was Kim Walters in the flesh. I knew that only because Stu called her darling. The big dark sunglasses, scarf covering her chestnut hair, and sloppy clothing were an effective disguise. She leaned out from the back-hall door before stepping into the front office space.

Stuart ran to draw the blinds, casting the room into a gray gloom. What is going on in here? Kim removed her sunglasses. She looked rough. Without her usual, carefully applied makeup, she was a different person.

"I know you are curious why I'm dressed like this. I've been in hiding, Jackie. The police are searching for me." A dramatic pause followed. "Please don't let anyone know you've seen me. I'll turn myself in soon."

"Kim, calm down. I think they just want to talk to you," I said.

"I don't think so. Murph told his mom Grace at the

coffee shop that they narrowed the list of suspects down. I'm a person of interest…I just know it. Plus, Stuart heard they have my evening bag, and they found it near the body. I left when you were still looking for it. You discovered the body. Did you find my purse, Jackie? You can tell me. Did you turn me in?"

"I didn't find it. No one turned you in, Kim. I think Murph or Jeff found it."

"And at the scene of the murder! I'm done for. I don't have an alibi either. I didn't do it but how can I prove that?"

Stuart turned to me. "Don't you understand Jackie? You must help protect one of our own against mounting evidence. I'll help too, but right now I have to get this written up for Tuesday's edition of the Harmony Hills Happenings."

Now it was Kim's turn to plead. "Jackie, you must remember how I helped you solved the Paul Griffin case."

Here we go again, I thought, but in order to calm her I simply agreed. "Yes Kim, you did. Now please, why are you so sure they blame you for the murder? Jeff is simply doing what is normal and asking questions of everyone who was there."

"It's not Jeff I'm afraid of. It's that detective woman. She has a mean look in her eyes."

"When did you see her?"

Kim back peddled. "I didn't actually see her, but she questioned Stuart at some length, and he didn't like her." She leaned against his stout chest. "Stuart likes everyone."

"When they discovered your evening bag in the room where it appeared Luella was murdered, they would want to speak to you, Kim. It's just how an investigation proceeds."

"Appeared? It appeared she was murdered there?" Stuart said. "But now what? They think she was murdered somewhere else and dragged to that room?"

"No. That's not what I meant. It's just that one can't assume anything. Will you two please get a grip?"

"We're trying," Stuart said. "And I also have a duty to get out the news…the facts, meaning I need to interview the detective and Jeff. But I'm afraid to. I thought you might have an in with them and can help me." He put his arms around his wife. "And her. Please just listen to her explanation of what happened, and you decide."

"Decide what?" I was beginning to feel strange about this. What did they expect me to do? Why didn't they just talk to Detective Taylor?

"I keep telling her, if you're innocent there's nothing to worry about," Stuart said.

Kim yanked away from Stuart's embrace. "I am innocent!"

"Of course, honey, I just worded that wrong. Jackie, please listen to her story and see if it makes sense to you. I mean you were right there in the middle of everything," Stuart said.

I knew what Kim was experiencing. I'd felt I was under a microscope with every question from Detective Taylor, like she suspected me too.

Stu said, "Kim, sweetheart, how about you take a deep calming breath. Pretend Jackie is doing the questioning. Tell Jackie everything you told me. It'll be like practice for when you talk to Jeff and that detective."

"Okay Stu. I'm better now that Jackie is here. First off, I think I know who did it...but let me save that for later. I was having a lovely evening in my new red gown. Did you like it?"

"Yes. You looked beautiful, Kim," I said patiently.

Kim's face tightened again. "Except that Ms. Hagge had to be there in the very same gown I was wearing. Who does that? I could have killed her when I saw that."

Stuart gasped and Kim's hand flew over her mouth.

"Honey you can't talk like that," he scolded her, tossing a pleading look my way.

"Kim, did you express those sentiments to anyone at the party that evening?" I asked, fearful how that would sound to someone if they overheard her. Especially someone who didn't know Kim's dramatic side.

Kim stuck her chin out. "I may have. But that's how I felt. Especially since she's the one who's messing with me, closing the deal with the resort developers who want to do work here. Every step of the way she has her hand out. Zoning needs to be changed. You need special water rights permits. Blah blah blah. I just can't stand her!"

Stuart's distraught look said it all.

I took a deep breath myself before continuing. "Kim you've got to understand that some people might take comments like those literally. Now back to what happened Saturday night. You were enjoying yourself until you saw Luella had the same gown as you. Right?"

"Yes. That's right. I'm not proud of how I reacted. But it was more than the dress. I had tried to reason with Luella for over a year. I'd heard about her accepting payouts, bribes, whatever people call those sorts of things, but I wasn't about to give her that. My reputation would be tarnished. When I pointed out Luella to Alan as being the head of the County Building and Zoning Department, he clenched his jaws and his fists. Maybe I shouldn't have brought her to his attention? His attorneys have been the ones dealing with her. He looked so angry. He pulled me aside and asked me to meet him in Eleanor's old office."

I remembered looking through the window at the office from the grounds outside. Had that been her talking with Alan? "So, what did he want to talk to you about?"

"He wanted me to get Luella somewhere private so he could confront her about what she'd been doing. He was going on and on about payoff, under the table dealings. Who did she think she was dealing with? This wasn't Cook County. That's Chicago, right?"

I nodded.

"Anyway, I think he'd had a little too much champagne. I'd never seen him like that. I know he's about ready to give up on the whole project, so I agreed to set it up. I discovered a quiet room to use. I waited for her to come out of the bathroom and asked her to join me, telling her that someone wanted to talk with her about the development and what he could do to expedite the process. She agreed, practically rubbing her greedy red-finger-nailed claws together."

"Take a breath Kim…," Stuart said.

"Sorry. Alan was waiting in the wings for me to text him and let him know it was a go. This sneaking around isn't in my comfort zone. I was nervous and wanted out of there. See no evil and all that. In the process I must have dropped my purse. I left her in the room and walked to the stairs. Then lights out and I fell."

"Did Luella and Alan meet?"

"Yes," Kim said, wide-eyed and holding her breath.

"Where, Kim? Where did they meet?"

"In the room where you found her body."

CHAPTER TEN

So, Kim knows that Alan, in an angry state, met with Luella in the very room she was murdered in. That is important information she's withholding. What I don't understand is why she doesn't just tell Jeff and Detective Taylor what she knows. When I questioned her about it, she couldn't give me a good reason. She mumbled about not being able to prove it. Who would believe her?

Did she expect Alan would lie? Stupid question I suppose. If he's guilty he'd lie to get out of it...most people would. Stuart and I both told her she had to go to the authorities. She finally agreed but wanted to go home first and pull herself together.

I left the newspaper offices, making Stu promise she would do what she said, and to let me know when she actually talked to the authorities, or I would have to talk to Jeff myself. He understood and agreed he'd get her there.

I sat on the bench outside the studio to think back to that time before the lights went out. Kim was there on the second floor, but I didn't see Alan. She told me she texted him to come upstairs just after she left Luella in the sitting room. We saw her come out of the bathroom.

Was she lying? Her purse was found in the murder room.

But what proof is there that Alan entered that small sitting room?

I knew I had to get this to Jeff. But it could wait for a little longer. Alan had already left town and Kim promised she'd go to the police station. She couldn't hide forever. She could change her story even. What I heard today would be considered secondhand.

I was pulled from of my thoughts by Ruth stepping out of the studio. "Hey there…want to take a walk with me? I'm on a mission to deliver a few of the raffle prizes from the drawing Saturday night."

Perfect. I would get some exercise and pass some time so Kim could talk to the police before I did. "Sure, where are you heading?"

Ruth referred to a paper clipped to the top of a folder. "Let's see. Hannah said she grouped these near here. A $10 gift card from the hardware store won by Bernie at the post office. And Stella over at the Farmer's Credit Union won a package of car washes. I've got a gift certificate to the Wildwood Supper Club for Ginger who works at the library. Mani-pedi from the Cut-n-Curl for Murph at the police station. Too funny! He'll go for that, I'm sure. Last stop the village hall with a super-duper prize of free ice cream cones daily from the Dairy Queen. So, tempt you with all of that?"

"Yes, Auntie you did. Let's go!"

It was fun and wonderfully distracting to walk the downtown area and meet the people who'd won raffle prizes. They'd purchased them to support the creation of the Harmony House and Museum but couldn't have afforded the ticket price of $100 to attend the event Saturday night. Ruth explained that every raffle ticket purchased included a free pass to the house in the future.

When we arrived at the police station to give Murph his gift, I noticed Detective Taylor and Jeff were meeting with someone in his office. "Here you go Officer Patrick Murphy. You've won a gift certificate. Congratulations!"

Murph eagerly reached for the paper. "Hope it's for the hardware store. I need a new set of allen wrenches."

Ruth, knowing what it was, didn't say a word. We

both watched his mouth drop open and started laughing as Murph absorbed what he'd just won.

"What's a mani-pedi?" He looked at us with a befuddled expression.

Ruth quickly explained, adding a suggestion that his mother Grace might enjoy it.

"Or do you have a girlfriend?" I asked.

"I am kind of interested in someone. But I don't think we're at the point I could give her this. It feels sort of personal like," he said.

"Did you meet her online? My friends are dipping their toes in that a bit," Ruth said.

Murph seemed stunned. Was it the question or that fact that my aunt, in her 80s, would even consider it? "No ma'am, I met her at the new brewery in town."

"Ah, the more classic way of meeting…at a bar," Ruth said. "How about the Chief? He's been divorced from Patti long enough already. Is he dating anyone?"

I knew why she was asking this. She hoped to light a fire under me to find someone. She'd been hoping this for years and I understood her point but had to smile at this suggestion. Though I shouldn't rule anything out, I guess.

"He's not dating anyone I know of," Murph answered.

Aunt Ruth tried to be funny, batting her eyes at me…

but I just shook my head and tried to engage Murph in more conversation. I was stalling hoping for the meeting to be over so I could tell Jeff to expect to see Kim today. But no such luck.

The meeting in Jeff's office continued. My curiosity kicked into high gear. "Murph, could I use your restroom please? Ruth and I have some more raffle gifts to deliver and well, you know..."

"Right down there, Jackie."

It was easier to sneak a peek into the meeting this way. It was Alan! That's a surprise. He must have driven over from Chicago this morning. They know something already or he wouldn't have been brought in for this in person interview. I bumped into the water cooler and gave an awkward wave as all three turned to see what caused the noise. Detective Taylor's stern look was balanced by Jeff's wave back at me.

I mouthed sorry and stepped into the rest room. Was Alan turning the tables on Kim?

Our final stop was the Village Hall. I asked Aunt Ruth about Patti and Scott's divorce. I didn't want to say something awkward since I'd be working with her daughter-in-law.

"Their divorce was amicable. Matt was over eighteen so no custody issues. Both good people."

"Any idea what happened?"

"Rumor had it that Patti married Scott on the rebound from her high school sweetheart who left for college. She found out her first love was dating while away and I guess she figured she'd do the same and picked Scott. Her high school boyfriend went on to earn a law degree and lived in another city. While here in Harmony Scott fell for her really hard and convinced her to marry him. Big mistake."

"Why, if they are both so nice and all?"

"Patti always carried a torch for her first boyfriend, and he for her apparently. He never married and when they found each other several years ago, the fire still burned."

"Patti cheated on Scott? I feel so bad for him."

"Nope she didn't. But Scott knew how she felt, and he didn't want to remain married to her, knowing she loved someone else. He released her from her vows, is what he told his son Matt and Matt told Mandy and Mandy told me. Isn't that just the most romantic thing?" Ruth said. "Scott is an honorable and very single man."

Again, with the hints!

The Village of Harmony had put a substantial investment into their new municipal center. The grounds were manicured and freshly mulched. Late spring tulips in vivid pinks and peaches spread along the edges of the flower beds. Hosta and daylily leaves were pushing out, ready to take over in a few weeks. The front desk person led us to Patti's office. She was a slender woman with bright hazel eyes and a welcoming smile. Dozens of family photos were displayed on the shelf behind her desk. An African Violet bloomed in her office window.

"How's my favorite photographer today?" Patti said, as she rose from her desk to greet us.

"I'm wonderful and I come bearing a prize for my favorite village administrator," Ruth said.

"I won something? Hooray!"

Ruth handed her the free ice cream punch card and introduced me.

"Very nice to meet you, Jacqueline. I so admire your work." She turned me around and pointed to a print of mine hanging on the wall behind me. A shot of the hills above the Wisconsin River in all of their fall splendor.

"Thank you, Patti," I said. "I remember that year. The autumn colors were astounding."

"And you caught them at their peak. The Farmer's Almanac predicts high color levels this year too. Do I understand you'll have a home here by then?"

"I will. Hopefully sooner," I said.

"Mandy tells me she'll be working for you. I'm so excited for you, but also for her. What an opportunity."

"I'm looking forward to it myself. She seems like a bright young woman."

"And a hard worker," Ruth added. "She's helping me clean out the old darkroom so she can set up a framing workshop there. I'm a bit apprehensive about what we'll uncover. That room has sat untouched for so many years."

"Does anyone even develop film anymore, Jacqueline?"

"Oh sure. Not the casual user. Digital photography, even in the phones we carry around with us, has eliminated the need for most film developing places. But there are still photographers who use 35mm and need to have it processed."

Patti stood up and called her assistant in. "Joyce, could you come in here please with that box of old film canisters? Jackie, do you know the nearest place we could get old film developed? We found some in a storage room. I don't know what's on them, but I hate to just toss them out. The Historical Society is searching for photographs to archive and display in their new home on Harmony Hill. There could be something on these the committee might want."

Joyce entered the room carrying a small box with

about twenty film canisters in it. "Is this what you wanted?"

"Yes great. Thanks. We've been wondering what we should do with these. The committee might find a photo or two in here to keep, but I wanted to have them developed first. I hope I don't have to send them off to Milwaukee or something."

"Patti, I'm not sure, but let me take those and I'll see to it they get developed. I can give them directly to the Historical Society?"

"No, I think we'd better take a peek at them first." Patti smiled apologetically. "I wouldn't want to embarrass some previous employees. I heard there were some wild and crazy Christmas parties and summer picnics back in the day!"

CHAPTER ELEVEN

Ruth and I, with our raffle prize deliveries completed, decided on the Harmony Diner for lunch. Dolly greeted us and seated us at a booth next to the window. This time we ordered the meatloaf special. Even with all the wonderful restaurants in Chicago, and the gourmet restaurants I've eaten in from Paris to Tokyo, I always look forward to a Harmony Diner special when I come to town. Real comfort food.

I noticed Chief Jeff and Detective Taylor having lunch in the corner. They seemed to be enjoying each other's company. I'm glad for him. He's such a nice guy. And looking like Jeff Bridges makes him pretty darn cute too. Plus the whole man in a uniform thing working for him too.

The detective left and Jeff appeared to be making a

phone call before paying the bill. Ruth had excused herself saying Mandy was waiting for her at the studio. I decided to stall and try to catch him to tell him about Kim, since he'd been busy earlier. Jeff might be willing to talk more freely without Detective Taylor. I know I would, because he wouldn't make me feel like a suspect the way she does.

"Hey Jackie. Nice to see you again and under different circumstance than a murder scene. Can you join me for a few minutes? I'd like to pick your brain about something," Jeff said as I approached his table. Perfect, I thought…I want to learn something from you, too.

"Of course, Jeff. Let me bring my coffee cup over here," I said.

Dolly appeared with the coffee pot and topped off both of our cups as I sat down in Jeff's booth.

"What did you want to ask me?" I said.

"I know you are curious how we ended up interviewing Alan at the station. Could I run through what he said with you and get your thoughts on it?"

This was too easy…it was exactly what I wanted to hear. "Sure, Jeff. I hope you won't get in trouble with the detective."

He grinned. "I might have to swear you in. Or are you okay with keeping this info confidential for now?"

"I swear I will. Can I first ask if Kim came in for her interview yet?"

"She is coming in after lunch."

"Now, what was it about Alan you wanted my thoughts on?" Secretly I was pleased he had turned to me.

Jeff began to tell me what Alan revealed at their meeting this morning. How he appeared shocked to hear about Luella and explained that he left very early Sunday morning for the drive back to Chicago and didn't even know about it until my office reached out to him.

"Did you believe that he hadn't even heard about Luella being murdered?" I asked.

"Knowing Kim, I'm surprised she didn't call him right away. He told us that he tried to reach Kim when he got back home to Chicago late Saturday night, but he got her voice mail and no call back. Which is the same for us. She hasn't talked to us yet, and she's a prime witness."

"I talked to her earlier this morning when Stuart asked me to come into his office. I made her promise she'd talk to you today."

"How'd she seem to you?"

"Physically all right, but she was very nervous. She thought you were going to arrive with handcuffs at any moment. She expected that coming to you would be tantamount to turning herself in. But please, go on about what you learned from Alan."

"He explained being surprised to see Luella Hagge at the party. His attorneys dealt with her. He'd never met the woman. Gorgeous woman but full of herself was one remark he made."

"Did he say what the lawyers were dealing with?"

"Apparently Luella tried the old tricks of suggesting campaign donations would help expedite resort permits and clear up zoning issues."

"Sounds like Cook County years ago," I said.

"Exactly. He figured that was pretty aggressive of her to try to strong arm his group. I felt he wanted to control the direction of our interview."

"Like put out his version of the night, in anticipation of you asking him if he spoke with Luella at the party?"

"Right. He volunteered to come in and give us his version. He claimed that Kim Walters pushed him to meet up with Luella. She could arrange a private meeting by having Luella go to one of the unused rooms upstairs. When asked why Kim would involve herself like that, he told us that she's been involved all along. Getting this deal through would net her a tidy commission. And he thought that Kim had an unhealthy appetite to see Luella dealt with harshly, as in reporting her unlawful actions to the board. But Kim was torn because that meant the deal would fall apart. A part of Kim wanted me to just throw in the towel and let money pass under the table or into Luella's campaign coffers, Alan told us. That if he supported Luella in her race, it might be enough to guarantee a final judgement before she left her current position with the county. Kim was right in that regard because Luella had something we both wanted…a ruling and soon. He said his investors would back out if this thing didn't get moving."

"Wow, you and Detective Taylor learned a lot in that meeting. So did Alan meet Luella for a secret powwow?"

"He said he didn't. But that he had a sneaking suspicion that Kim might try to implicate him, because she was so adamant that he meet with Luella. She had texted Alan which room Luella was waiting in just before the lights went out and she fell down the stairs. He explained that's when the whole thing fell apart and he offered to drive her home. He said he didn't want to get caught up in all this small-town garbage…let the lawyers handle it."

"Well now Mr. Chief of Police…what are you going to do with all of that?"

"That's where you come in. I want your thoughts on

this. You were upstairs and saw Kim's mood, her behavior. Did you see Alan?"

"I didn't see him. And Kim's mood felt a little off. Which would be explained if she knew Luella and Alan were meeting just feet away from us."

"Or explained by her having just whopped a heavy vase against the back of Luella's head?" Jeff said, a concerned look on his face.

"So, Kim is a suspect then?"

"We have several persons of interest. And yes, Kim is one of them."

"One thing I didn't mention when I spoke to you and Detective Taylor on Saturday was that I saw what might have been a meeting in Eleanor's office between Alan and someone in a red dress. I was standing in the yard looking back at the house. A figure paced in the room and because of the uneven gait I assumed it was Alan. He seemed very animated. I caught a brief flash of red. Knowing what we've found out today it might have been Kim."

"Was this before you and Hannah went upstairs?"

"Yes, before," I confirmed.

"That could have been where Kim pushed Alan to talk directly to Luella like he said."

"Right. I agree. I just don't think Kim could have murdered Luella. About Alan…I don't know? Maybe he did meet with her and struck out in a moment of anger?"

"Kim and Alan aren't alone in disliking, even hating Luella Hagge. Lou and I have been inundated with information about how many enemies she had, including builders and developers she upset. Rumors are flying about her taking money under the table to grant zoning changes or expedite permits. And Alan's story certainly confirms that. Plus, any attorney who litigates cases makes enemies along the way…and Luella did that for years."

I couldn't help but notice Jeff used Detective's Taylor's nickname again. I suppose that was normal in the law enforcement field.

"Let's keep in touch, Jeff. Especially after you've had a chance to talk to Kim. I've got to run now. Senator Bennett's wife had the highest bid for my photography session. They asked if we could do it at the Harmony House today."

"Betsy was upstairs at the time the lights went out too, wasn't she?"

"Yes, remember I told you that when you and the detective interviewed me on Saturday?"

"Right, would you mind letting me know if you see or hear anything from Mrs. Bennett today that might be helpful?" Jeff said. "We'd appreciate it."

. . .

While I was at lunch, Mandy and Ruth had torn apart the dark room. The front studio was full of sorting boxes, odd pieces of equipment, and feather boas!

Feather boas? Looking more closely I discovered what appeared to be red silk pantaloons. Is that what these are? I held them up against me. Yes, it would appear so.

"Now don't you look cute in those?" Ruth said, laughing as she carried a file box out of the old dark room. She stopped to survey the piles of things now in the studio. She proceeded to push some things together with her foot and put the box down. "No idea that room held so much!"

"Easy Auntie watch out for your back," I said, twirling one of the boas around my neck. "What is all this stuff?" I stepped over boxes and around a velvet chaise lounge.

"This is the accumulation of years of work here. I'm having such fun discovering all the props and backdrops buried away. That thing wrapped around your neck belonged to the time when taking boudoir photos, to give your husband of course, was a fad. Now they'd be laughable. What teenage girls wear is more come hither than any of this stuff. But I do remember a couple of the gals I photographed showing a little more skin than I might have expected."

"And Dad took those photographs?"

"For heaven's sake, Jackie. No, he didn't. Women around here would have been way too embarrassed to do that. I took the photos."

Mandy walked out carrying a shoe box holding film canisters similar to those from Patti. "I wonder if these are any good."

Ruth grabbed the box from her. She checked the canister dates. "I wonder how these got overlooked?"

"When were they from?" I asked.

She put the cover back on the box. "From the 60s. They probably can't even be developed anymore."

"Well let's try. I've got the ones from Patti, remember. I'll take these too." I reached for the box, but Ruth pulled it back.

"No that's all right. Probably just junk or we would have developed them."

Mandy asked, "Patti gave you old film? From what?"

"I guess photos someone took at village events. I'm going to check into getting them developed when I get back to Chicago," I answered.

"Randomly I know of a place in Greensville that still processes 35mm film. Why don't I run them up there later today? I could take yours too, Ruth," Mandy offered.

"No really. I'd rather not waste the money," Ruth said.

"My treat, Aunt Ruth. How about we take one and see if it shows anything?"

Ruth hesitated again. But Mandy and I waited, and she finally relented and handed over one of the old Kodak canisters.

"I'll run them over after the photo shoot at the house. That way, maybe I can pick them up tomorrow," Mandy said.

CHAPTER TWELVE

Mandy and I left for the Harmony House. She was grateful for the hands-on experience and I was glad she was so willing to take on this learning opportunity. Scott's pickup truck was parked alongside a work van with Hanson's Electric written on the side. Scott and another man walked out of the house just as we pulled up.

"Busy day here," Scott said. "I see you're working my daughter-in-law pretty hard. What are you two doing out here?"

Mandy gave Scott a quick hug. "Jackie is going to let me help photograph the senator. His wife won the bid for Jackie's package at the auction Saturday night."

Scott's neatly groomed gray mustache almost hid the little grin he gave Mandy. In his wonderfully deep rich voice he said, "Hope you don't go taking off for the big city lights and life like she did."

"You and Matt are stuck with me staying in Harmony," Mandy said, "But I've made him promise we'll do lots of traveling." She timidly ducked her head. "At least until our family gets too big."

"Now that is music to my ears! Grandchildren? When?" Scott exclaimed.

"Whoa…slow down. Not for a few years." She held her hand up. "I've got to get my career established first."

Scott winked at me and said, "Well then I'll be sure to get going on that remodeling at Parker Photography so Jackie here can get the new look she wants, you two can build up the business, and I can have grandchildren!"

I laughed at his timeline. "Sounds like a plan!"

"I understand you met my ex?" Scott said.

"I did. Ruth and I were delivering raffle prizes and Patti won a year's supply of ice cream cones. You two will make great grandparents when the time comes. But I see something else coming now, my appointment. I mean our appointment. Come on Mandy, let's get set up."

I began explaining some things to help Mandy. "Besides the technical things, like aperture stops and shutter speed, a portrait photographer needs to get a feel for the people she's photographing. Put them at ease, you want them to be themselves. On that topic, I can tell we have two subjects who are not at ease."

"Agreed," Mandy whispered to me. "I sense a tenseness in their body language."

"Good call."

"Hello Jacqueline," Betsy greeted me. "I'm sorry we're late."

"No problem, Mrs. Bennett. I'd like you to meet my assistant Mandy Drake."

"Nice to meet you, dear. I wasn't aware of a prior appointment my husband had so I'm afraid our time will be cut short. Have you met my husband?"

The Senator obviously was not happy to be here. Betsy wanted to find out what progress had been made regarding the investigation, but her husband's impatience with the discussion was obvious.

"Robert, aren't you the least bit curious about who murdered Luella Hagge?" Betsy asked.

"Why should I be? I never met the woman before Saturday night," Robert announced in a don't-question-me voice.

Betsy exchanged a direct look with him. "Hmm...I didn't know her, but I thought you had met each other, dear. Are you sure?"

Neither Mandy nor I missed his angry glare, but

Betsy deflected it by quickly turning her face to the sun. "Isn't this a wonderful day to be outside?"

I picked up on her cue to move along on the outdoor shots. The sun wasn't at the best angle, but this would have to do. We used a low rock wall and the thick trunk of a tree as props.

After taking a few shots, Betsy said, "Shall we go in now? I'd like photographs on the staircase. It's so dramatic."

We hurried to catch up with the Senator who strode ahead of us. "I wanted to compliment you on your gorgeous evening attire. With your height and slim figure, you wore that simple white silk blouse and full skirt so elegantly. On me it would look like I was one of those crocheted dolls on the toilet paper roll. I bet you don't even remember those, do you Mandy?" Betsy asked.

"No ma'am, I don't."

I said, "Why thank you. I wanted to compliment you on that perfume you wore Saturday. Red Door by Elizabeth Arden, right?"

"Yes. Oldie but goodie."

"It was so nice to meet you on Saturday. By the conversation you had with Hannah you and your husband must really enjoy antiques and antique shopping," I said.

"I do, but Robert not so much. He and I don't have a great deal in common. I could barely get him here for this photo shoot with you, as you can tell. I've admired your work and was excited to bid on your package."

"Thank you, Betsy. I'm glad you won it. Here we go. The grand staircase."

"Can we finish up?" Robert stood waiting inside the front door.

I gave guidance to Mandy regarding the placement of the camera to avoid the refracted light from the stained-glass windows. I posed Robert and Betsy explaining to Mandy the why's of each position.

We'd gotten several shots and were just repositioning our camera for a new angle when Senator Bennett said, "Excuse me, but could we wrap up here? My wife wasn't expecting to be part of lessons for an amateur on our time," Robert snapped.

"Robert!"

He huffed and clenched his fists.

"Sorry," Betsy said, as something behind me caught her eye.

I turned and there stood Detective Taylor leaning her hip on the entry door frame, her arms crossed on her chest. Watching us.

"When you're finished, I'd like to have a word with you, Mrs. Bennett."

"Excuse me, but you are who?" Robert asked in an arrogant tone.

She pulled out her badge. "Detective Louise Taylor."

"Well Detective Louise Taylor, my wife and I are in a hurry. And we were just finishing up here. Am I right?" He shot me daggers.

"I understand, but it shouldn't take long. If you prefer, we can meet at the local police station."

Betsy turned a worried look toward her husband. "It's all right. I'll talk to her."

"Robert demanded to know why his wife should agree to talk.

"She was at the scene of a crime and I have a few questions for her. I've been calling your office but apparently your staff isn't giving you the messages. I would hate to think you consciously chose not to return my calls."

"I saw no need. My wife and I left the party early. Didn't we?"

Betsy meekly nodded.

"This way please, Mrs. Bennett. And Mr. Bennett, would you mind waiting outside?"

Well, guess this photo shoot is over. I prepared to pack up my equipment, but Detective Taylor asked if I would mind joining Betsy and her up on the second floor.

"I've got it, Jackie," Mandy said. "You go ahead."

"Now Mrs. Bennett, the reason I wanted to talk to you is that I understand you were here on the second-floor landing during the time period we have established for Ms. Hagge's murder. Is that correct?"

"Yes, I was here. I came up here to use the powder room. But I don't know about any time period."

"Was that all you came up here to do?"

Betsy stammered. "Let me think. I may have checked out some antiques that were on display in the rooms."

"You were in rooms other than the powder room? Do you remember which ones?"

"No, I don't. It was a busy evening. My husband is a Senator you know, and we were busy."

"Yes, I know him, Mrs. Bennett," Detective Taylor said. "Ms. Parker, when did you first notice Betsy was here?"

I wanted to be careful. This woman unnerved me. What had I told her before? The truth. But one's memory doesn't always remember the exact complete same truth day to day.

"I believe I first saw her when Hannah and I came down from the third floor. We were using the back stairs." I tried the knob of one of the hall doors to show her. But it wasn't the right one. I chose another and was relieved when it revealed the staircase.

"I see. Just to clarify, Betsy was in the hall outside this door when you first encountered her."

"Yes."

The bright yellow crime scene tape secured across the door across from us. It couldn't be ignored. At least for me. I noticed Betsy averted her eyes, keeping them on the floor at her feet.

"What was Mrs. Bennett's demeanor?" Detective Taylor asked.

I looked at Betsy, but her eyes were still on the floor. Had she been in a room with Luella? It was right across from us.

"Ms. Parker, please answer my question."

I took a deep swallow. "She seemed a bit confused. I asked her if she was lost and she laughed in a nervous way."

"All right," Betsy spit out. "I was in that room." She pointed to the door behind which Luella had been murdered.

"Did you see Ms. Hagge in the room? Did you speak with her?"

I couldn't believe my ears when Betsy said, "That hussy? You bet I spoke to her. But I didn't kill her."

"That's not what I'm asking Mrs. Bennett. Please calm down and explain what happened."

"I was in there and we argued. When I left the room,

she was sitting in the same chair as when I found her. Her hands with her perfectly red manicured nails draped over the arms of it. Her legs crossed with the slit of her skirt falling open. It took all I had to say my piece and walk out."

"What did you tell her?"

Betsy clammed up and snapped back into control of herself. "That's personal, and I'd rather not discuss it here."

"It might help if you told me," Detective Taylor said.

"It had to do with the way she treated my husband. She's a rude and nasty person."

Detective Taylor didn't let up. "Did you see anyone in the hall when you left the room?"

Betsy seemed surprised that she wasn't pressed further on what had occurred between her and Luella. So was I, but then I'm not a detective. I would have wanted to know why the burst of anger.

"I was flustered and confused, just as Jackie said. I was turned around. I heard voices and didn't want anyone to see me in this state. But I couldn't just stand here so I pulled myself together and walked back toward the landing pretending I was lost and looking for the powder room."

"Thank you, Mrs. Bennett. Please keep yourself available for further questions." She handed her two cards. "And give this one to your husband or whoever screens his calls. We really don't have time to be chasing down witnesses like I had to do today. Good day Mrs. Bennett…Ms. Parker."

"Betsy, I'm so sorry, but I had to tell her the truth. Are you okay?"

"No, but I'll be better once I get away from this place." And she practically ran down the stairs and out the door.

Why had she argued with someone she'd never met? Where did that moment of rage come from?

CHAPTER THIRTEEN

I heard the Historical Society meeting going on in the parlor of the Harmony House tonight. Second time here today. It was hard to believe that mild-mannered Betsy Bennett had said what she did this afternoon. It left me puzzled and I'm sure that Detective Taylor felt the same.

I peeked around the dark wood frame of the cased opening. Apparently, I was late. I'd taken a nap when I got back to the studio and Ruth left me a note that the gals were picking her up for this meeting. She included a suggestion that I might enjoy joining them tonight.

Hannah, standing at the front of the room with everyone's focus on her, noticed me and said, "Come in please, Jackie. Everyone, this is Jacqueline Parker, Ruth's niece. I'm glad you came, because I wanted to explain to the committee the idea we discussed briefly on Saturday."

I knew some of the faces that turned to look at me. Aunt Ruth's friends, Dorothy, Eunice, and Betty from Shady Pines gave me big smiles and waves. Eleanor was here too. I was glad to see her and hoped we'd get a chance to catch up after the meeting was over.

Two elderly men sat on folding chairs next to each other. One with his legs stretched out in front of him and his unruly beard resting above his crossed arms. The other balding with reading glasses perched on his full bulbous nose, his eyes darting around the room. The balding one introduced himself as Elmer Fisher and pointing to his friend said, "This wily old man is Harry Cooper."

A woman closer to my age smiled and moved over on the damask settee she occupied. "Hi, I'm Kay Whitlow. Welcome to our meeting."

And of course, I knew Mark and Hannah from Sutton's Antiques. Hannah held up a clipboard. "We had a great deal of interest in more people joining our committee now that they've seen the projects ahead of us. Some signups from Saturday evening are for temporary volunteers to finish getting this place ready for opening. I'm excited to read a name or two willing to help with putting up a website for us too. That'll be critical to be able to reach tourists and for special seasonal events. The website will have to be updated frequently and I'm hopeful one of them will be willing to build it and maintain it as well."

"What about a lawyer volunteer? Bet Kim will sue us for her fall," Elmer said.

"People round here don't sue over such things," Eunice snapped.

"Wouldn't be so sure about that missy," Elmer retorted.

I could well imagine Eunice didn't appreciate being called missy.

Hannah raised her hand to hush them. "He has a fair point. We are working with an insurance agency to acquire appropriate liability and property insurance. And…," She put her reading glasses on, flipped the signup sheet over, and peered down at the next paper on her clipboard. "Dane Berryman did donate twenty hours of legal service, valued at $4000."

"He ain't worth that much," Elmer mumbled as Harry snickered.

Dorothy shook her head. "For god's sake, Elmer. Let the man donate what he wants. Doesn't cost us anything. What else was donated, Hannah?"

"I'll pass the clipboard around for everyone to read. It has the signups, donations, plus raffle prize winners and high auction bidders. The community really stepped up. Okay, let me see. We've run through the funds raised by the silent auction and the raffle. We still need to wrap up finding the winners as our drawings were closed down by an unfortunate event and guests left early."

With a dismissive snort, Eunice said, "I can see why. Finding a dead body will clear out a party pretty quickly."

Uncomfortable giggles rolled out across the room.

Hannah shrugged. "Yes, I'm afraid we ended the evening on a somber note." She raised her pointer finger up in the air. "But on a high note, the power going out was attributed to an overload. A new electric panel was included in Scott's bid, so that shouldn't be an additional expenditure. And I was told our own Jacqueline Parker already delivered on her donation. She photographed Senator and Mrs. Bennett this afternoon right here at the house."

"Ohh la-la. You get to photograph Robert," Betty giggled. "He's such a flirt, but in a cute way."

"He's full of himself," Eunice said.

"No, he's not," Betty remarked. "He's an important person. They're not all pompous. He just exudes confidence."

Dorothy said, "He seems like a decent sort if you like that type."

I leaned over to ask her, "What type?"

Dorothy winked and cupped her hand to whisper in my ear. "A pompous flirt."

"May I ask how it went for you, Jackie?" Hannah said.

I decided to gloss over the end of the session and simply said, "Fine. I'll be getting prints to them soon."

"Wonderful. I hope they'll agree to us using them in some sort of promotion and on a Facebook page we'll be setting up."

"He'll put up his face anywhere anyone lets him," Eunice said.

"Our meeting is digressing. To get back on track I'd like to announce the plans that Jackie and Mandy from Parker Photography have agreed to work with us on."

Hannah explained the idea she had of doing an extensive book on the large wardrobe left behind. "The garments are in amazing condition. They are carefully packed to prevent moth damage. Most are even tagged with who they belonged to, any special events it was worn at, and where it was purchased. For instance, many of you may remember when Ruth's sister-in-law ran the *Vogue on Main* dress shop in town. Some garments carry her label. It will be a project for the future, but we are excited about it. Jackie, would you like to say anything?"

I felt funny being asked to speak again. "It's something I look forward to working on, partially because I'll be setting up shop here in Harmony. I don't know if Ruth has already told you all, but I'm taking over our family photography studio."

"What are you going to do with it?" Kay Whitlow asked me.

"It'll still be a photography studio, Kay, but also a gallery for my work and that of other photography artists. Mandy Drake will be doing custom framing. In fact, Hannah has been stashing antique frames for us to use. I'm remodeling and hope to have it open for the height of tourist season. I'd love to have an exhibit promoting the Harmony House."

Hannah was all smiles, and she gave me a big hug. "I'm so happy to hear that. Let's have a round of applause to welcome Jackie's business to our village."

I basked in the faces and smiles in front of me. My Aunt Ruth and her friends. Dear sweet Eleanor.

Hannah next called on Eleanor to address the group. "I'm here to share with you how delighted I am with the progress being made on taking Harmony House forward. She has sheltered and protected my family for generations, and now her beauty will be enjoyed by generations to come. I have such fond memories here." She paused. The audience knew she had some sad ones as well.

"I remember celebrating birthdays with pony rides and clowns, even though my parents knew I was afraid of clowns. I think they agreed with the saying to face your fears. As I grew, I brought young men here to meet my parents." She softly chuckled before continuing. "Several young men. Even married some of them! And there were a few my parents never met because they snuck in via the trellis."

Laughter from the audience and a few shocked expressions. "I'm very excited to watch Hannah catalog the wardrobes of my family over the years. I can't say thank you enough for the pleasure I'm receiving from the wonderful care you've all given my gift to the Village of Harmony. I'm sure it will be a gift that keeps on giving."

A round of applause followed as Eleanor returned to her seat.

Kay was asked to address the committee on the ongoing reconstruction and remodeling project. "Scott has let me know he is running into several delays in getting permits and variance or zoning. Things are held up in the county. But we keep on pushing and should accomplish everything as we've outlined it."

"With Luella gone there will be no paying for faster service," Elmer said, followed by yet another loud snicker from Harry. Was that another attempt at humor? I couldn't tell.

Ruth reported on the progress of gathering historic photographs to archive in the Harmony House Museum. "We are so appreciative of the abundance of photographs donated. Some are in need of repair. Mandy is working with that process…mostly digitally. It's really quite something. I think everyone will be pleased. When the website is up, I'd like to share those in which we can't identify the people. Myself, Dorothy, Eunice, and Betty have polished off many a wine bottle in pursuit of the truth…getting a name to put to the face from the past. And we bravely forge forward with our efforts."

Ruth got a rousing round of applause and shouts of *We'll help* and *Hard work, but someone has to do it!*

Elmer reported that a large pumpkin patch was already planted. Suggestions for using the nature preserve for a fall festival and a Halloween celebration were given and noted.

Eleanor suggested a haunted walk through the nature paths that were being developed. "If it works, I would love to see part of the mansion turned into a haunted house. I always wanted to do that, but mother never allowed it. That way the ghosts we have here can join in!"

Eunice couldn't resist throwing out the suggestion that a resident ghost pushed Kim down the stairs.

Eleanor asked, "By the way, how is Kim? Has anyone seen her since Saturday?"

I made the decision not to volunteer that I had. I wanted Kim to give herself time to show her face. Besides, I had the clipboard holding the winners of the raffle prizes in my lap and I was skimming it for the number series of the ticket stubs I found under the vined trellis. I found that one of them had won a prize. It was claimed by the bartender at the Wildwood Supper Club. Congratulating Lynn on her win would be a good excuse to go to the supper club…as if I needed one. I texted Wanda if she wanted to meet there tomorrow night. She responded instantly.

You don't have to ask twice, 7:00? See you there tomorrow.

CHAPTER FOURTEEN

On Tuesday morning I woke thrilled to begin discussing the changes to the Parker Studio I'd been dreaming about. And to meet my old, both in age and length of friendship, friend Wanda for a goodbye at the Wildwood when the day was done. Thinking about the fact that while I'm back in Chicago, a home and business will be worked on for me was exciting.

Scott Drake was the only local contractor I wanted to work with…not only because he was easy on the eyes and Mandy's father-in-law, but because he came highly recommended. He arrived promptly at ten with a notepad and tape measure.

"Good morning, Jackie. How are things with you this fine day?"

"Morning Scott. I'm so excited to show you my vision for this place. Want to start down here first?"

"Sure. How did the photography shoot go yesterday?"

"It was interesting to say the least. Did you see that Detective Taylor caught up with Betsy Bennett? A few fireworks there. Ended with Betsy practically running out of the mansion. Have you heard anything more about the investigation?"

"Not really. I guess my main contribution was that the electric panel didn't malfunction."

"So, someone did tamper with it?" I was surprised to learn this.

"No. It functioned just as it should when it's overloaded. The lights, the band in the solarium, the kitchen…all those circuits drawing juice. The old panel wasn't set up for that and shut down. I've got the new one with more amps installed. That's one thing I wanted to check on here today. Might be quite a few things that need updating. This building must be over a hundred years old."

"At least something here is older than me."

"And me," Scott said. "I don't imagine I'll ever slow down, I love my work and it's what keeps me going. Oh, and the possibility of a grandchild!"

"I'm so happy for Matt and Mandy. Such big things ahead of them."

"Is there a husband back in Chicago that will be joining you out here?"

"No. Never married. So, I don't have the grandchildren thing working for me. And I'm an only child so no nieces and nephews. But I have some second cousins in the area and I'm an honorary auntie many times over."

"Hard to believe a beautiful woman like you never caught the right man's eye."

I laughed. "I caught a few eyes in my day. And my eyes did a little catching as well. I found a few good men, just not into the forever thing. Guess I'm in the generation when so much started changing. Marriage wasn't the most important thing to many of us. My career was my first love. Marriage and children weren't in the cards for me. Have you remarried, Scott?"

"Nope. Once was enough. I've had some ladies in my life since Patti and I divorced, and we've enjoyed each other's company." He offered an embarrassed smile. "But enough about us baby boomers. Show me your ideas. Renovating this space is going to be a fun project."

I felt the same. Scott's enthusiasm was contagious. I was ready for this new phase of my life in Harmony to begin. We started in the front of the studio. I explained my concept of a gallery type display. "I'm not sure how much the historic designation downtown here will inhibit the facade. But if we're lucky, I can enlarge the front window area."

"I'll check into that, but if we can't put in bigger ones, these current display windows will have to do."

The dark room that Mandy and Ruth had emptied out yesterday was next. "I want this room to be used for framing. Mandy had a great idea to add a custom framing element back to what Parker Photography Studio offers. Frames complete the image the camera creates. Too often the images don't even get out of phones, much less framed for display. We'll need storage on this wall and a large worktable. Maybe two tables. I want good lighting…no more of those dark room red safelights."

Scott had some great suggestions about the office and storage areas, plus the back entry. "I see your aunt doesn't use these stairs much." He pointed to the leaf filled outside staircase that went up the apartment. "I'd like to see this enclosed. It appears there's a good depth to this alley. We might be able to buy some of this adjacent property and tie it in with a heated garage. You are planning on keeping living quarters for yourself upstairs, right?"

"I am. Let's head up there now."

Aunt Ruth had a fresh pot of coffee waiting for us. I

showed Scott how I'd like the old apartment updated. Open concept in the living area. Enlarge the bath.

"A bit more luxurious?" he asked.

"Yes. I like a good soaking tub."

Ruth put her hands over her ears. "I don't want to hear this. I won't even want to move out when I see the changes you're making."

"Aunt Ruth, I'll send Scott over to the cottage you're buying at Shady Pines and add a soaking tub there. My treat. Consider it a house, I mean, cottage warming gift."

We went over everything, and Scott promised he'd email me some plans. "Matt is learning the AutoCAD program, maybe yours can be the first 3D rendering for him to do."

"I'd love that! I'm leaving Thursday, but here is my business card with my email address."

"Leaving so soon?" he said.

"Yes, but once this space is completed, I'll be here much more."

Ruth added, "I'm trying to convince her to move her base of operations here. Wish me luck with that."

Scott teased her. "I do wish you luck. Believe me."

. . .

The Harmony Hills Happenings Tuesday edition should be out by now. After saying goodbye to Scott, I went to Stuart's office to see if he and Kim were okay. He wasn't in the office and the red and white closed sign hung in the window without explanation. No *I'll be right back,* or *Gone for coffee* note attached to it.

Today's papers were in a stand just outside the door, so I grabbed one and took it to the nearby park to read the article about Luella's murder. Stuart, in defiance, had put the article about the fundraising gala on the front page along with three of the photographs he'd captured that night. He detailed future plans with quotes from some local attendees and one of the renderings Scott had presented. I wasn't aware of how much property was going along with the donation of the house. Very generous of Eleanor. Stuart wrote of the nature preserve plans to include extensive hiking trails with signage. Even a small bunk house being built to be used by school groups and scout troops.

I turned the page to finish the article, and that's where I saw a small headline reading, *Luella Hagge Murdered.* The words that followed reminded me of that old TV show where the detective said *Give me the facts ma'am, just the facts.* That's not what Stuart had done. In the beginning of the article, he walked readers through Luella's career and her current running for the district attorney seat. Then he dipped into some rather unsavory, and in my opinion, unnecessary verbiage, including a short list of cases she handled as a private attorney. Was he trying to make her look bad and thus less sympathetic? The Horton Street building collapse lawsuit, a suit against a local bank for fraud, a Greensville deli run out of business by a civil lawsuit she brought for a client. They were worded to imply that these were questionable settlements.

I looked up and saw Stuart walking along down Main Street. His head hung and his usual happy gait was replaced with an odd shuffle. I called out, but he didn't hear me. He began to unlock his office door but stopped, turned away from it, and took the side street that led uphill. I hurried to catch up. He trudged up the gentle incline ahead.

What's wrong? What's happened? Do I approach him, or does he want to be left alone? I made the decision to reach out to him. Maybe he just didn't feel well. He might need help.

"Stuart, wait up!" I shouted at the top of my voice.

He heard me this time. "They've arrested Kim," he said in a monotone voice and with fear-filled eyes. "Can you help her?"

"What? That can't be true! This was way too quick. Why would they do that? Kim's not a flight risk. And here I thought they were shifting focus to Betsy or Alan. Stuart, let me buy you a coffee from Grace. I could use one too. We'll go back to the police station together."

"I can't. I need to go home and try to find an attorney for her. I need to get bail money. Jackie, Kim's been charged with first degree murder. She didn't do it."

"I know she didn't. I'll go over there and see what I can do. Are they holding her there?"

He nodded, turned, and continued on toward his home.

CHAPTER FIFTEEN

I hurried back down Main Street and over to the village municipal complex which included the police station. The sprawl of green space surrounding it was being cut and that wonderful fresh grass smell slowed me down. The world out here moved on in the way a normal Tuesday morning would in a small town. Grass cutting, shoppers walking, boats riding on the water. But behind the doors in front of me, someone's life was at stake.

Could Kim have done this awful thing? I immediately thought no, but was I missing something? In anger might she have swung that vase at Luella? No, it just didn't compute for me.

I pushed on through the doors and ran into Detective Taylor leaving. "Sorry, excuse me," I said.

"We meet again," she said under her breath as she passed me. I stared at her back as she walked to an unmarked vehicle and pulled away.

Jeff stood behind the tall front counter. "Morning Jackie. I assume you've heard about Kim."

"Oh Jeff. This can't be right. Did she make it in yesterday?"

"No, she didn't. She was still refusing to come and talk. I found her at the newspaper offices this morning. I imagine she thought if she just ignored it, it would all go away. The County Sheriff has been pushing us to make an arrest. He needs to make an impression to keep his position this year. Everything points to Kim. Threats made at the party. Admitting she was with Luella in the room. Finding her purse there. The timing with you and Hannah seeing her and her being obviously upset. We just don't have any other good suspects."

"I don't remember calling her upset in my interview. At least not the upset she'd be if she'd just hit someone with a two-pound vase. What about Alan?" I asked. "He was going to meet with Luella too."

"He denies he did though. And no one saw him up there. Someone would have seen him go upstairs at some point."

"Jeff, there's a back staircase. Couldn't he have used

that? The room Luella was in was on the side hall, out of sight from the main landing."

Jeff's eyes shifted slightly. "I suppose. But there was no reason for Alan to hurt Luella. And you know how volatile Kim is. The charges might be lowered to second degree since it wasn't premeditated."

"Can I see her?"

Jeff said, "Give me a minute." He walked down a hallway that I assume led to the jail cells. This was surreal.

He soon came back and ushered me through a heavy door. In the last of three small cells Kim stood. She looked as good as always. Not like the Kim I saw on Monday. Crisply pressed slacks with a cream silk blouse. Her nails were still the vivid red she'd had on Saturday night. What gave away her mood were her eyes. In them I saw the terror of what she faced.

Jeff asked her to step back, and he opened the cell door. "I'll leave this open and check back on you two in a few minutes."

I nodded and stepped inside the small, enclosed space. I'm glad he left the door open.

Kim remained mute. Probably still in a state of shock. I reached out and pulled her to me in an embrace. "Sit down, Kim. I spoke to Stuart. He's getting you an attorney and will have you bailed out shortly."

Kim finally spoke. "Thank you, Jackie."

"Is there anything I can do to help?"

"Turn time back." She broke down sobbing.

I let her cry until the sobs died away and she sat upright. "You've got to help Stuart. He's going to try to investigate on his own. It has to be Alan who did this. It has to be. But I don't know how we can prove it."

I didn't either but I knew she needed some comforting words. "I will try Kim. I have some connections in Chicago from knowing his old partner, Paul. Maybe I can find out something that way." I left her there promising to assure her husband Stuart that she would be okay and would be waiting to hear from him.

Once outside the police station I sucked in a full breath of the clear clean spring air. Mandy was walking up to the village offices. She waved me over. "I picked up the developed film from the guy in Greensville. I dropped off the one packet for Ruth, not sure how those turned out. And I'm just heading in to give these to Patti. Looks like they developed just fine. Not the high depth of current shots but pretty darn good." She pulled out one of the packets to show me. "This one looks like a village Christmas party from years ago. I can tell by the fashions and hairdos."

I took them from her and tried to show enthusiasm, which was hard to conjure up after where I'd just come from. In the third photo I noticed Luella. A younger Luella. She wore red again, which made sense as these were from a Christmas party. She was not the focus of the photographer. It obviously was the group of three people in front of him holding toasts of wine up for the camera to capture. Luella and her companion were not trying to be seen, in fact they probably thought they were out of range of a camera. But they weren't. She seductively pressed her body against a man who didn't seem to mind.

"Are you heading back to the studio? I'll walk with you if you can give me just a minute to get these to Patti," Mandy said.

"I'll go in with you."

As soon as we were in Patti's office, I showed her the one with Luella in it and asked if she knew the man.

Patti took it and pulled a magnifying glass from her desk drawer. "The tool of boomers," she said with a chuckle as she held it up to the photo. "You recognized Luella. She worked here for a short period. And the man might be Bob, our district attorney at the time. Those were some interesting parties. Things have toned down a bit since then."

"Bob who?" I asked.

"Bob Bennett, our current state senator."

"May I take this photo please? I'll return it."

"Keep it. I don't think it's something he'd want to be shown around. But why do you want it, Jackie?"

"I'll explain later. It might help with the investigation." Then I told Patti and Mandy about Kim's arrest. "She's sitting in a jail cell as we speak."

"You've got to be kidding! I know Kim. She's a little over the top sometimes, but a murderer? No way," Patti said.

Jeff was in his office when I returned to the police station and dropped the photograph on his desk.

"The Senator lied about knowing Luella and this proves it."

He took the photo in hand. "Where did you get this?"

"It came from Patti's office. Old photos that got misplaced and never developed until now."

"So, what does it prove? We didn't ask him if he knew her. Lots of people knew her. Besides when would he have told you that?"

"Yesterday. I did a photo shoot with him and his wife Betsy at the mansion. She bid on it at the auction and her bid won. He was not happy to be there, and he let everyone know."

"I don't get it, Jackie. This sure has you fired up. Just tell me what you're thinking."

"That Luella and Senator Bennett had an affair and his wife Betsy learned about it. She admitted to Detective Taylor that she was in the room with Luella at one point. You can ask her yourself," I said. "Seeing the photograph puts the whole thing with Betsy in perspective. This is why she confronted Luella. Not some other lame excuse she gave Detective Taylor. She was a wife tired of covering for her husband's affairs."

"Lou told me about the conversation she had with Betsy yesterday and that you were with them. How did that come about?" Jeff asked.

"Detective Taylor asked me to. But in a conversation with myself and Mandy, the Senator said he'd never met Luella Hagge. But then his wife said Luella had treated her husband badly. One of them is lying."

"We didn't interview the Senator. You say Mandy can corroborate what he said?"

"She can. He's lying." I pounded my fist down on the photograph lying between us. "And this proves it. You asked me what I think. Well, I think you should talk to Betsy again. Passion is powerful. You've got to try. This was almost too easy to arrest Kim."

"Calm down Jackie. That's not fair to say. You think I want to see one of our own behind jail bars? I don't. This wasn't any easy thing to do. I'll see what more I can find out without involving Detective Taylor. She doesn't have to know until I get something more definitive than your hunch about an affair," Jeff said.

"Sorry Jeff. But I'm so sure it's not Kim. In fact, she's asked me to try to find out more about Alan. I believe she thinks he did meet Luella in the room and lost his temper. But she can't prove it. I'm not saying it's Betsy, but I am saying both Betsy and Alan deserve more attention."

"Jackie, I agree. Lou seemed to accept Betsy's reason for talking to Luella and believed her story about Luella being alive when she left the room. I think we should spread the word that Kim's been charged. It might loosen tongues here in town if people think the case is solved."

CHAPTER SIXTEEN

It had been a long day, and I looked forward to meeting Wanda at the Wildwood Supper Club for drinks. A bar stool to sit on, an Old-fashioned to drink, and a friend to talk with, just what I needed tonight. I'd asked Ruth to join us, but she declined saying she was going out to the new Stone Mill Brewery with the girls to celebrate her moving to Shady Pines. I still get a kick out of hearing that name. I always think of the old TV show The Golden Girls when Dorothy would threaten her mother Sophia with the line *Shady Pines, Ma...Shady Pines*…to remind Sophia about the nursing home option!

The bartender Lynn remembered me from the last time I'd come in and even remembered I'd ordered a Whiskey Old-fashioned sweet. Wanda ordered the same.

Neither of us was very hungry, so we opted for shrimp cocktails to nibble on at the bar.

"I'm still so shocked about Kim being arrested," Wanda said. "That's unbelievable. She wouldn't want to take the chance she'd ruin her nails by swinging a heavy vase at someone."

"Ouch! Feeling snarky tonight, Wanda? Where did that come from?"

"Sorry. It's just that she's been in everyone's face trying to get us to all fall in love with this resort coming and I say sure, but enough already. Sometimes she's just so overbearing. Always checking herself out in the nearest reflective surface."

"I know what you mean. But I find her amusing and endearing. Plus, I'm doing this for Stuart. He is madly in love with her and he's just out of his mind with worry."

"Doing what?" Wanda asked.

"Trying to find other possible suspects. He's certain it isn't her. Since I'm in town, I may as well do what I can."

The bartender, Lynn said, "Are you talking about Kim Walters? She can put on airs but she's just trying to make a living. Real estate isn't easy, and you have to present yourself in a certain way to attract attention and be remembered. Were you guys up at the house Saturday when that Hagge lady was murdered?"

"We were," Wanda said, pointing at me. "In fact, this woman found the body!"

"OMG! Wow that's crazy." Lynn turned to call out to some customers who pushed their empty glasses in her direction. "Hold your horses down there."

Wanda said, "Go ahead Lynn. We'll be here for a while."

"Excuse me…you'd think they were dying of thirst." Lynn slid away to pull a couple of draft beers. The customers wore business suits, but with their ties undone. I couldn't help but feel they would be having a liquid dinner tonight.

"If you believe Kim didn't do it, who did?" Wanda asked me.

"I have a couple of suspects, but apparently Detective Taylor is set on Kim," I said. "You remember Alan Morris? He stayed in one of your cabins for Eleanor's wedding. The one that didn't happen. And he was with Paul Griffin before that tragic auto accident."

"Sure. But why would he be involved with Luella?"

"Luella Hagge is the Building and Zoning Department head for the county and is, I mean was, apparently trying to do some dirty under the table dealings with Alan's attorneys to get money for granting permits and variances." I reached for a cold shrimp and dipped it in the cocktail sauce before taking a bite. "At least that's what Kim claims."

"Whoa…that's interesting. Have they questioned this guy?" Lynn was back in front of us. "I thought that corruption only happened in big cities. We're just a small village. Another round for you ladies?"

Wanda pushed our empty glasses toward Lynn. "Yes, we will have another. I think my friend has some more to share with us."

Lynn carefully muddled the orange and sugar cube together before pouring the whisky in. "So that would take the heat off Kim, right?"

"You'd think," Wanda said.

"They did interview him, and seems they believed his story. He said sure Kim tried to get him to meet with Luella, but he never did. He figured why should he? Let the lawyers handle it. But Kim still claims he did go to meet Luella. Except no one seems to have seen him even go upstairs, much less enter the room her body was found in," I explained.

Wanda raised her new drink. "Here's to figuring out a way to take the heat off Kim. Too bad all that happened. The evening was mild, the moon was full, the ladies were all beautiful, and the men were all handsome…a perfect party."

Lynn pointed out that it wasn't quite perfect.

"Gripes just go with it, Lynn," Wanda said. "It's too morbid to keep bringing up the fact that the whole evening ground to a halt when the lights went out and someone was murdered."

"Agreed," Lynn said. "On a lighter note, I won a raffle prize! A year of free carwashes at the Suds and Go."

"I didn't see you at the party," Wanda said.

"I wasn't there. No way could I afford one of those $100 tickets. But I did know someone who was going to be there, and we chipped in money and he bought us raffle tickets. Except I was pissed when he ended up losing the ticket stubs. Can you believe it? Didn't matter though because he wrote our phone numbers on each one put in for the drawing. Some nice old lady called and then showed up yesterday with my prize."

I remembered randomly seeing that prize on the clipboard at the meeting Monday night. The number sequence caught my attention because of my birthday connection. Just like the ones Libby had found at the base of the trellis. But how did they end up in the bushes in a hidden corner of the mansion? "Lynn, who went to the party and bought the tickets for you? A customer from here?"

"No. Me and Pete from here and the other three from the brewery. Pete set it up because he tends bar part-time there too. One of the waiters works side jobs with the caterer who did the event."

Wanda said, "That caterer did a great job! Didn't she Jackie? The food was..." She touched her fingers to her lips and popped them with a smack. "...perfecto!"

"All so professional too. The wait staff in nice crisp white shirts and black ties. Real crystal champagne glasses. Beautiful china serving pieces," I said.

"Yes, it was a lovely evening until...well the lights went out," Wanda said.

"Back to that again?" Lynn said. "I take it that's when the murder happened. Sounds like a novel or a board game. Was there an inspector twirling his handle-bar mustache and smoking a pipe as he solved the mystery?"

"Could have been, but I didn't see him. We just have my handsome cousin, our Chief of Police," Wanda said. "Is there someone else you suspect, Jackie?"

Lynn had to excuse herself again, but I was intrigued by what I'd just learned.

"I do have another suspect, Wanda, but I'll save that one for now. Do you mind if we stop in and check out the Stone Mill Brewery?"

"I know that look on your face, Jacqueline Parker. There's more to it than stopping for a beer. What's up?"

I laughed. "Ah my friend you know me well." I made a quick decision to share my happy news with her, because she was my friend and because it would distract her for the time being. "Aunt Ruth is there celebrating my buying the Parker Photography Studio from her."

"What? Girlfriend, you didn't tell me that. Happy dance time." Wanda skipped and twirled to her car, shouting, "Whoopee!"

She was one of the reasons I looked forward to spending more time in Harmony. I hoped the remodeling wouldn't take too long. Summer on the river sounded wonderful.

As we drove to the brewery Wanda explained the uptick in activity in the area. "Businesses are starting to come here in anticipation of that condo or resort development finally happening. The brewery got this great location. Remember the old stone building on the edge of the river? I think it was a paper mill. Perfect for a business like the brewery. And right on the river. Now all the talk about a walking path along the river might start turning into action."

This end of town was the manufacturing side of Harmony. Many of my classmates' fathers had worked in this paper mill at one time. It was good to watch towns, including Chicago, able to save and repurpose sturdy old buildings by putting in lofts or businesses. I was happy Harmony had done the same. It added a new vibrancy to my hometown, and my photography gallery would fit right in. But my excitement was tempered with the poignancy of knowing the small-town feeling might be diminished with progress.

The Stone Mill Brewery was busy for a Tuesday night. A perfect song played at just the right volume, Creedence Clearwater Revival's *Bad Moon Rising*. One of my favorites growing up. I liked this place already. They had an appreciation of good music.

I asked, "Is Shorty losing business with this new bar in town?" Shorty's was one of the local taverns. From my balcony at night, I heard his jukebox playing as customers walked in and out, opening and closing doors. It had been Shorty's when Wanda and I went to high school and tried to sneak in…as did many other teenagers.

"He's good with it. His clientele is sticking with him and he's even selling craft beer from this brewery if you can believe it. There they are." We wove our way through the tables to where Ruth sat with her friends.

"What a great surprise!" Ruth cried out. "Do you remember Rocco Montalvo? We met him at the fundraiser."

Rocco rose and pulled up two chairs for us while Betty and Ruth slid over to make room.

"I don't believe we were formally introduced. Your aunt was kind enough to invite me to her celebration. I understand you will be taking on her business here in this lovely little village," he said as he flagged a waiter over and ordered another round of drinks for everyone.

When the waiter returned with our drinks, I noted he added more water to Rocco's glass. He saw me watching. "It's been my pleasure to chauffeur these lovely ladies on this celebratory evening. I'm officially their designated driver."

Even Eunice giggled at that and Eunice rarely giggles! "He lives in Chicago too, Jackie. Just like you. Isn't he the dearest?"

"How is it you ended up at a fundraiser in the hills of Harmony?" Wanda asked. "I remember almost bumping into you at the party. You did some smooth quick steps to get out of my way."

"And I remember you looking lovely in that stunningly patterned gown. I attended the event because I noticed fliers posted in the marina. I felt it a worthy cause for a town I want to spend more time in."

"Are you planning on moving here, Rocco?" I asked.

"I'm considering it. I'm here working right now, and I plan on keeping my boat in the marina for the summer to get a good feel for the place. After this pleasant evening with these young ladies, I'm even more certain the summer will be enjoyable."

"Two evenings with us lovelies," Betty reminded him, leaning coyly toward Rocco.

Rocco winked. "I stand corrected. Jacqueline, your aunt mentioned you have a loft in River North. Great area of the city."

Aunt Ruth chimed in. "Rocco is heeere oon business."

Oh boy, she's going to sleep good tonight, I thought as I detected a slight slur in her words. How long had they been here? I was a little leery of this Rocco character. What was he doing hanging out with these four? My curiosity prompted me to ask him, "What is it you do?"

"I'm here on behalf of a group of businessmen and women from Chicago who are interested in investing in this area. Sort of scouting, you might say."

There was a unique properness to him. Was there still a mob presence in Chicago? He had that vibe for some reason. The finely dressed and properly mannered thug.

"He used to be a Chicago detective, didn't you?" Betty said. "Isn't that something? A real-life big city detective in our little town."

Rocco smiled. "Not a detective, Betty. I'm sorry if you misunderstood me. I work with detectives. I'm more of an investigator for private enterprises."

He's an investigator? For private enterprises? Exactly what does that mean? Pretty broad and ambiguous terms. But on a more practical note, I could use someone familiar with Chicago to check further into Alan Morris. I've only seen Alan here twice. And both times he was in the circle of people involved in a death. Might be time to get a better sense of Alan's life outside of Harmony. I'd try to keep an open mind about Rocco…maybe he could be useful.

But first…I was here for a different reason. I left the table with the excuse of using the restroom. Stopping at the large horseshoe-shaped bar I found someone who appeared to be an owner or manager.

"Good evening. Enjoying yourself?" he asked me as I walked slowly past with the purpose of engaging him in conversation.

"I am. You've got quite a place. A big addition to Harmony."

"Thank you. Yes, we're still new, but doing well. Looking forward to summer with boating and tourists. Hope they get that river walk path completed soon."

"I noticed you donated prizes to the fundraiser on Saturday. Thank you for that."

"Were you a part of putting it on?"

"Peripherally."

"Tough hearing about that woman being murdered. Puts a damper on the evening."

"Yes, it did. Did I understand you were involved in

the catering too? It was wonderful, and I'd like to congratulate you."

"Us? Catering? No, we weren't part of that. We're a pub food kind of place. Not what they wanted."

"Hmm, I must have heard something wrong. I met a nice waiter, and he mentioned this brewery briefly. I must have put two and two together and come up to three," I said with a self-deprecating laugh.

"I heard one of our guys worked that party for some extra money," he said.

"Would he happen to be here? I meant to give him my card to contact me for a possible gathering I'm planning."

"I think he's around." He leaned across the bar and called to one of the bartenders. "Hey Pete, do you know where George is?"

Pete came over. "He left early. He has a long drive home."

The manager's shoulders went up as if to say sorry can't help.

"Oh, where does he live?" I asked.

Pete looked at me directly. "Who's asking?"

"Don't be rude to our guest," the manager said. "Just answer her question."

"I'm sorry. I just found something he may have dropped at the event he worked on Saturday."

The bartender looked at me oddly. “I overheard you say you were looking to hire him for something.”

"That, too,” I said quickly, trying to cover my mistake.

“I don’t know exactly. Sorry.” Pete spun on his heel and walked away.

I quickly shoved one of my cards out toward him. “In case you see him, please give him this.”

He glanced at my business card, then looked across the room to where the celebration of the sale of Parker Photography was going on.

“You the lady buying that business?” He jerked his head in the direction of Ruth’s table.

“Yes I am.”

“Why do you want to find George?” Pete asked.

“Like I said, I found something that I think he might have dropped at the party.”

“Leave it here. I’ll get it to him.”

Sensing his resistance to me I figured it was better if I backed out of this conversation. “I didn’t bring it with me. I didn’t even know he worked here until I talked to Lynn at the Wildwood. No biggie. I’ll be in town another day. Thanks for your help.”

CHAPTER SEVENTEEN

The sound of breaking glass.

The scream of the store alarm.

Libby barking wildly.

I bolted up from the couch and ran into Ruth coming out of her bedroom.

"What's going on?" she cried.

"Something broke the window downstairs, and that set off the alarm. Does it go right to the police station?" I found myself yelling above the alarm wailing around us.

"Yes."

I looked out the balcony's glass door. From this vantage point I couldn't see anyone running away. I stepped out and looked down. Nothing. The glass must have shattered inward, meaning someone might be downstairs inside the studio. Or had thrown something and fled.

"Can you turn off the alarm?" I asked.

Ruth appeared confused, pushing at some buttons on a pad near the stairway.

The alarm kept ringing.

Libby kept barking.

I reached for her collar and made her sit. At least that stopped one of the loud noises.

It had to be after midnight. Finally, Ruth silenced the alarm and the police sirens started up.

No sounds came from directly below us. I felt it safe for me to go downstairs. Unless a burglar waited in silence, which I doubted. He would have fled by now.

The whirling colors of blue bounced off the light posts and trees outside and into the ceiling of our second-floor apartment. Taking three steps down, the blue whirling lights revealed the damage to the studio. It appeared someone had thrown a projectile in. Broken glass covered the floor just inside the window.

Flashlights shone in from an officer on the sidewalk. I saw his hand resting on the gun in his holster.

Not wanting to startle the officer I called out. "I'm here with Ruth Parker. May I come down?"

He pointed the beam directly in my face. "I see you. Come down with your hands up ma'am."

I did as he directed though I thought it was a little overkill. “Let me unlock the door and let you in. Wait, a minute. I have to go back up and put on shoes.”

“Stay where you are. I’ll come through the window.”

He kicked one lingering pane of glass in, which cleared the space for him to step over the window ledge. He fanned the flashlight beam around the room. “Please go back upstairs while I check the place. I’ll give you the all clear and you can come down then.”

By the time he gave the all clear, Ruth and I had robes and shoes on. We were able to assess the damage. It was only broken glass. Nothing appeared to have been taken.

The officer introduced himself and said the Police Chief was on his way.

Jeff arrived dressed in blue jeans and a sweatshirt. I resisted the urge to run and give him a hug. I was so relieved. His familiar face comforted me.

Jeff picked up a large rock holding a piece of paper rubber-banded tight to it. His gloved hand carefully removed the banding, and he opened the note. His eyes scanned it, before looking up at me with concern deepening the lines in his face.

. . .

*o back to Chicago. Keep away.*

"What's going on Jackie? Is there something you're not telling me?"

"No Jeff. I'm as shocked by this as you are."

"Jackie, think. Have you been doing some investigating on your own again? I seem to remember you going off the range before and visiting Cutter at the salvage yard."

"Yeh but…"

"Obviously this message was directed to you, Jackie. Any ideas why someone would send you this?"

He had me there. What had I done that warranted this? Was the Senator upset with me telling the detective about his wife being upstairs? Or was Rocco really not here for the reason he said? Might Alan actually be using him to scare me off?

"Come upstairs. We'll put on a pot of coffee and talk. I'll run a couple of things past you."

As the coffee brewed, I filled Jeff in on what I'd found near the base of the trellis. And how this evening might lead me to learn who dropped the raffle ticket stubs at the base of the vine. I asked for his help with two things and he grudgingly agreed but not without issuing me a warning. "Jackie, I'll give you tomorrow, but then I take this to Detective Taylor. Agreed?"

"I understand. Thank you. This could be a wild goose chase and I appreciate you keeping it between us for now. Sounds like the cleanup crew is here."

The police had called a 24-hour service to clean up the broken glass and board up the window.

Needless to say, Ruth and I didn't get much sleep.

CHAPTER EIGHTEEN

After a long hot shower, I was ready to call Rocco. I needed to address this head on in the bright morning light. I got his number from Ruth and he agreed to meet for breakfast at the diner. He was already there waiting when I walked in, and apparently had gotten to know Dolly. She certainly was a hub of social life here in Harmony.

Dolly heard about the rock coming through our window too, but not about the note. Rocco didn't know about the note either, but saw the plywood covering the studio windows and was eager to hear what had happened.

I showed him a photo of the note.

"Do you know what this might mean?" I asked him.

His face was immobile, but he slowly turned his dark

eyes to me. We held our stares until he spoke. "I'm not surprised by your question. It did take me some time to think through why you linked the rock to me. You believe Alan Morris is involved in it?"

So, he does know Alan Morris. I was right on that point. I'd suspected that might be the case. "I don't know who did this. But I sure want to find out," I said. "As to why I asked you, let's just say ever since we crossed paths outside at Harmony House on Saturday night, I've had mixed feelings about you. You are very suave and entertaining. You dress in expensive well-fitted clothing. I don't know a great deal about cigars, but the Cubans you smoke are expensive and very hard to come by. You describe yourself as an investigator. I guess my curiosity won out and made me call you."

"But you didn't answer my question, Jacqueline. Do you think that I'm working for Alan Morris and that I had some thug do this dastardly deed to scare you off? Everyone knows you want to find the murderer to help your friend Kim. Am I right?"

I tried to keep a poker face, but he really assessed my situation well. I had to be careful, he seemed ready for me and my questions. "What or why I'm asking questions doesn't matter. But you didn't answer my original question. Do you know who did this?"

Rocco leaned toward me, his elbows resting on the

table. "I don't. Now answer mine. Do you think I work for Alan and want to pull any suspicions away from him by scaring you off?"

"It did cross my mind."

"First off, I don't work for him. In fact, he's a part of what I'm investigating for the group I was hired by."

Inwardly I was relieved. But I needed to confirm that what he was saying is true. How could I know he was telling the truth? He must have read my mind.

"I can understand why you might not believe me. But you will see I'm telling the truth in good time. And that will have to do. May I continue to speak candidly and in confidence?"

"Sure. Go ahead." I decided I'd let him tell me whatever he wanted, while I would be careful to not say too much to him.

"I've been keeping my ear to the ground about the lags and delays on the resort deal Alan Morris and Paul Griffin had been trying to put together. When Paul pulled out, and subsequently died, Alan kept assuring the investors he could still put it together. But time was passing, and they hired me to use my discretion in finding out what was happening in Harmony. Let's just say they have their suspicions about Alan."

"Have you found out anything unsavory he might be doing?"

"You mean like killing Luella Hagge to get her out of the way?"

I didn't answer.

He continued, "I'm still not sure about Alan's innocence. I learned about Kim Walters and Luella Hagge and the antagonistic feelings they have. I know Kim has been arrested for the murder, but I don't believe she did it."

"I don't either. On that we can agree."

"That leaves a couple of others. Betsy Bennett and Alan Morris," Rocco said.

"I won't even ask how you know about Betsy, but yes they are in my radar as well." I stopped there, not wanting to tell him about the third possibility I'd brought to Jeff's attention last night.

"If I were you Jackie, I'd look seriously into the Senator. He and Luella had a torrid affair that his wife knew about. It's over. But Luella threatened to reveal it if he didn't throw his wholehearted endorsement behind her. She was a power-hungry woman who uses then discards people. Now it appears someone decided she needed to be taken out. Someone who is not locked up sent you a warning. I warn you, be careful Jacqueline. Luella messed with some powerful people. And she's dead. If Betsy did kill Luella, the Senator would want her protected because that would also protect him."

I was speechless. How did he know all of that? I suspected something like it, but he stated it as fact. Who was this man?

He saw my puzzlement and simply said, "I do a thorough job for my clients and Luella is part of it, because Alan kept blaming her for the delays. Time is money. My understanding is that Detective Taylor is not focusing on anyone but Kim. She's making a mistake."

"It appears she is. She's under a great deal of pressure from our County Sheriff to put this case to bed. Why should I not believe you are trying to misdirect me, Rocco?"

"Like I said, you will know in good time. I understand you have an inquisitive curious mind. I will warn you again, be careful with your curiosity. Remember it killed the cat."

Now what was that supposed to mean? It felt eerily like the threat from the note with the rock.

Rocco's eyes shifted sharply away to the entry door of the diner. Detective Taylor and Jeff stood there. "I will talk to you later," he said to me out of the corner of his mouth as he put on a relaxed face and waved at them.

They stopped at our table to say hello. I introduced Rocco without explaining how we knew each other. I knew I'd be talking to Jeff later, and I didn't want to complicate anything now. I needed to put a few things in order first.

CHAPTER NINETEEN

My first destination after leaving the diner was back out to the mansion. I knew Scott was working there today, and I needed his help.

"Hi Scott, how's your day going?"

"Better now," he said with a slow grin. "What can I help you with?"

"Could I borrow one of your ladders? There's something high up on a trellis in the back of the house that I need to see."

Scott carried an extension ladder and followed me to the hidden corner where the trellis stood. The corner where Libby had discovered the raffle ticket stubs.

"Right here will do," I said.

Scott leaned the ladder alongside the tall trellis.

"What is it you're looking for? I don't see anything unusual…just ivy leaves."

I couldn't see the odd object I'd seen earlier from up above. Fingers crossed it was still there. "Can you hold the ladder? What I'm after might be hidden behind them."

"How about I go up and look for it?" Scott said.

"No, I think I'd rather you held the ladder for me."

"You got it," he said. He braced himself on the ground and gripped the ladder, pushing his weight against it.

I knew it would be awkward having him looking up at me as I climbed, but in my day, I've been shown at worse angles. I just hoped what I'm looking for is still here.

It is!

I climbed back down and saw Scott's *what's up with that* look when he saw what I'd pulled out of the leaves.

"I'll explain later. Will you be out at Ruth's new cottage at Shady Pines today?"

"I will. In fact, Matt's out there with Ruth now doing some measuring and I was planning to leave in a few minutes."

"Great. I'll drive over shortly. I'm finding myself getting more and more eager to see her there so you can get started on the studio and my new home."

"Me too," he said, hoisting the ladder across his broad shoulders and walking it back inside the house.

There was a voice message waiting for me when I got back in my SUV. Rocco asked me to give him a call. I decided to wait until I'd talked to Jeff at the station. I hoped Detective Taylor wasn't there. But she was. That stymied the conversation I'd wanted to have with him.

"I'm sorry to hear about what happened to your aunt's place of business," Detective Taylor said. "Is she all right? That must have been quite a startling thing to have happen late at night. Have you given more thought to who might have left that message for you?"

"Not any more than what Jeff and I talked about last night." I knew I was being evasive, and I hoped Jeff had honored my request to keep our late-night conversation between the two of us for twenty-four hours in case I was way off base.

"That's too bad. He couldn't get any good prints from the scene and doesn't have much to go on," she said.

I decided to throw her a challenge. "Will you be going ahead with your charges against Kim?"

"Why wouldn't we? We don't even know this incident last night has anything to do with Luella's murder.

I've been considering it might be the fact that you are buying a small local business and trying to put in what some locals call a fancy gallery in its place. Wouldn't be the first time that citizens who don't like to see big changes to their way of life take action. I've noticed yard signs here suggesting just how many people oppose the development."

"That possibility hadn't crossed my mind," I said. And I thought it was a silly suggestion, but I couldn't tell her that. At least it gave me a little cover, a little more time. It also meant Kim would still have murder charges hanging over her, but that couldn't be avoided. "But back to the murder investigation. Are you following any other leads?"

"Of course, we would if we had any serious ones. Jeff, you were just mentioning someone recalled seeing a figure running past Kim just before she fell."

"Right," Jeff said. "Kim felt she was pushed. Hannah had a memory of a flash of white just before the lights went out. She and you both remembered hearing footsteps during the black out."

"When she brought in seeing that flash of white, we decided it was more of her eyes trying to do a quick adjustment to the sudden darkness," Detective Taylor said. "Do you recall seeing it, Ms. Parker?"

"I don't, but I was facing in a different direction. At

the historical society meeting Eleanor mentioned ghosts in the house. Maybe that was what she saw?"

"Could be," Jeff said.

"Just kidding! Come on…"

"A murder is hardly a joking matter. I'll be in touch, Chief. Good day, Ms. Parker." Detective Taylor spun on her heel and walked out.

"Why do I get the impression she doesn't like me?" I said as soon as the door closed behind her.

"She does have an edge to her. But like I said, she's under a lot of pressure from the sheriff. I'm afraid Kim Walters is headed for a trial. And sooner rather than later. Lou was, to put it mildly, displeased that you are injecting yourself in our investigation. She's hellbent on getting Kim to trial and the distractions you present irritate her."

"What distractions?"

"Lou got a call, and so did the sheriff, from Senator Bennett. He was extremely angry at the manner In which she'd pressured his wife on Monday. He said she did nothing wrong, and it was totally unnecessary that she be treated in such a disrespectful manner. He also felt your presence during the interview was inappropriate and violated his wife's privacy."

"I was there, Jeff. It didn't happen that way. Besides, the detective asked me to stay with her and Betsy."

"I'm just telling you that's the kind of pressure Taylor is under."

Now I was getting angry. "I can't help that. But it's not right to charge Kim so quickly either. Can't you slow your Lou down?"

"My Lou, as you call her, is in charge at this point. Unless you bring me some hard evidence, my hands are tied."

"Did you get the information I asked you to?"

"Hold on, Jackie. First who was that man you were having breakfast with?" Jeff said.

Should I confide in Jeff about Rocco? Maybe he could run a quick background check on him. Make sure he was who he said he was. Jeff listened and agreed to do the check. I also went ahead and shared what Rocco had told me about the Senator and Luella having had an affair.

"And he did that unprompted? It's the conclusion you came to also, isn't it? Now I can understand why the Senator got so riled up."

"It was pretty intense. Betsy did get shaken up, but Detective Taylor's line of questioning wasn't out of order. I'm not an investigator, but I felt she left Betsy off the hook. She changed her initial story and then admitted she'd been with Luella in the room before the lights went out, but Detective Taylor didn't pursue it."

"Lou mentioned that to me. She believed Betsy Bennett's explanation. Said it seemed to fit with what others told us. Look Jackie, we both know this wasn't some upset citizen threatening you about buying a business here. You are getting close to the truth about someone or they wouldn't have done that. I'll do that check on Mr. Montalvo, but first let me show you what I found out for you, and then you have to tell what it means."

I read over the printed list of names Jeff handed me. "Jeff, I really appreciate this. It doesn't mean much as it is. But I'll get back to you soon. Promise…gotta run now."

As soon as I left Jeff's office, I headed a couple of blocks away, leaving my vehicle at the village center. It was quicker to walk. I went to the offices of the Harmony Hills Happenings newspaper. Stuart looked glum, with a gray pallor to his face.

"Jackie, what on earth happened at the studio last night? I picked it up on the police scanner. Are you and Ruth okay?"

"We're fine. I will admit we were both a bit rattled when the crash woke us up…the alarm started that awful racket it does…and then on top of it, my new little buddy, Libby, began a protective barking. It was all quite chaotic. But all's well now. I don't know if you heard but I'm buying the business from Aunt Ruth, so I'll be remodeling, anyway. We're going to shut down the studio for a couple of weeks and put up a sign. That boarded-up window will just become part of the project."

"You're making light of this, but why would anyone do that?"

"I don't know. But it was a cowardly act. Throw a rock through a window with two elderly people and their little, but very cute dog, sleeping upstairs."

"Jackie be careful," Stuart said as he rose to get a coffee for me. "Now what was it you called about that you wanted me to investigate? I must say I will enjoy the distraction."

"How is Kim?"

"Not good, but she got bailed out this morning."

I handed him the list of names Jeff had provided me and explained what I'd like him to do.

"Thanks, Jackie, for including me in what you're working on. I've been going crazy feeling like there was nothing I could do to help Kim. Now I can investigate this for you and maybe even clear my wife in the process," Stuart said.

"It's just a hunch Stu. I hope we don't come up

empty-handed. I'm going out to Shady Pines now to check on some work Ruth is going to have done on the cottage she's buying."

This brought a big heartfelt smile to Stuart. "Oh, I'm so very happy to hear she got a place there. That was one of the best ideas for that old Lutheran campground. To set it up as a retirement village was perfect. I was wondering what was going to happen to the apartment Ruth lived in when you took over the business. Will you be staying there more now?"

"Yes. Scott Drake is working on both floors. I'll have a home here."

When I left Stuart's office, I called Rocco back.

"Jackie, I gathered further information on Alan Morris."

"I didn't ask you to do that."

"I took it upon myself because I knew it's what you wanted but were afraid to trust me enough to ask."

He was right. And I still was unsure about him, at least until Jeff showed me the results of the background check he promised to run as soon as I left. If it showed Rocco wasn't who he claimed to be, all bets were off.

"May I tell you what I found out?"

"Go ahead," I said as I turned my SUV on to Main Street pointed in the direction of Shady Pines.

"First let me say that I let my current clients know what is happening here. I speak to them frequently of course, but now I requested they question Alan directly. Alan confirmed that he spoke to Luella Saturday night at the fundraising event and did go to the meeting Kim had arranged."

"Really? That's interesting since he so flippantly denied it to all of us here. Go on…"

"He promised them that things will go smoother. Luella will no longer throw up roadblocks. It was a rather crass way to view a death in their minds."

"Ugh. What a sweet guy!"

"He admitted he met Luella upstairs. That she asked him why he wasn't married. Was he on the Chicago's most eligible bachelors list? He claimed that put him off. Was she flirting, hoping for an even bigger payout? He assured us he behaved like a gentleman. But that she got upset when he told her his only interest in meeting with her was to figure out what could be done to wrap up her issues with the resort project. She flew off the handle. He called her a big fish in a small pond and told her she better be careful who she angered. That she was playing with the big boys now."

"Ouch, I'm sure she wasn't used to being talked to like that. What happened then?"

"Sounds like it went downhill fast and he left the impromptu meeting. But not before grabbing Luella's wrist as she reached out to slap him. She was steamed but still alive when he left the room."

"That's quite a confession on his part."

"Agreed, but the man has lied to my group before. However, I believe he thought this tale would impress and convince the group. They assured me they remained stoic and didn't speak. Alan, realizing his words didn't have the intended effect, begged them to please give him some more time. That things are back on track now."

"So, are you doubting his confession? That it was just for show?" I asked.

Rocco paused, so I asked again, "Rocco do you believe what Alan told your group?"

"I'll reserve my opinion, Jackie. If you do the same."

CHAPTER TWENTY

Two pickup trucks with Drake Construction painted on the side doors were parked in front of the cottage Ruth now owned. Aunt Ruth's old Subaru sat in the cottage's small drive. Garages in the rough cedar style of the original campground cabins had been built by each residence to accommodate the seniors moving into the cottages.

Scott and his son Matt stood in the kitchen area with Ruth when I entered. They both seemed to tower over her. The scale here felt doll like. Perfect for Ruth. All on one level. Near friends. This made me happy.

Fresh pine smells came in through the open windows. Lemon oil scents floated near the built-in wooden shelf next to the front door. Whoever did the changeover from cabins to these lovely cottage homes must have kept original pieces when they could. This shelf might have held duffle bags, or sports gear. Wide and generous, I pictured Ruth putting her framed family photos and the handcrafted pottery she made at the senior center.

"Excuse me," I said. "Is the lady of the house in?"

Ruth exclaimed, "Jackie! I'm glad you're here. Matt has some terrific ideas to update the kitchen and bath for me."

She looked absolutely giddy. What a change in her life and a big one for me as well. "That's wonderful Auntie."

Scott patted his son on the shoulder. "Looks like you have a handle on this Matt. I'll be right outside. Jackie, could I talk to you for a minute?"

We both stood just outside the front door. "Look, Ruth even has a view of the river from here," I said. "Perfect. She'll be so happy. Have you met her friends who live here?"

Scott nodded. "I did on Saturday night. They seemed to have a blast at the party. I saw they even got some dancing in."

"I saw that."

"Jackie, I wanted to ask you if everything is okay? You said you'd explain later about what you found at Harmony House. Why were you in such a hurry to climb up that trellis? And then you dashed away like a woman on a mission."

He wanted answers I wasn't yet ready to give him. Why couldn't I just tell him what I thought? Instead, I said, "Just something about the night of the party, a few loose ends."

"Come on, I don't go out of my way to hold ladders for just anyone. Are you worried about Kim and trying to find something that will prove she didn't do it?"

"Something like that."

"It was a strange evening and I'm sorry I didn't get to see more of you there. Did I tell you how wonderful you looked?"

I felt a blush rise up on my cheeks. "It was so nice to see all the dressed-up guests."

"Guess no sweet talking on my part will make you give me an answer. That's all right, but I want you to know that if you need anything, just give me a shout. Even if it's only to hold a ladder for you again."

"That's nice of you Scott, thank you."

"Jackie, Ruth told me about the rock coming through the window last night. If it was meant to warn you off, you better pay attention. You're a big city person and think you've seen it all. But in Harmony it's unusual to have this sort of thing happen." Scott took me by the shoulders and looked directly in my eyes. "It's one thing to have you brush me off about what you found, but someone threatening you prompted me to have my electrician put up security cameras in both the back and front of the Parker Photography building today."

The catch in my throat meant I didn't get to thank Scott before Matt and Ruth came walking out and Scott's hands slipped back to his side.

"All done here for now Dad," Matt said. "I'm going to take Ruth to our cabinet maker and let them work out a finish color and hardware for her new kitchen. Ruth was telling me about the fun they had at the Stone Mill Brewery last night. Want to take your favorite son and his wife for dinner there later, Dad?"

"We'll have to make it another time. I'm meeting with a new customer tonight. Why don't you two go and have a night out on me?"

After Scott and Matt pulled away, I let Ruth know I had a couple more things I wanted to take care of today. That I might not be back in time for supper tonight.

"That's fine. I'm having supper here with the girls tonight. There's a potluck in the community center the first Wednesday of the month and since I'm close to being an official resident, I've been invited to attend."

"What dish are you bringing?"

"I'm running home and whipping up a tray of my deviled eggs."

"Yum…can you leave some in the refrigerator for me?"

"Of course, Jackie. I'll do it because I love you, but also because I owe you. You really figured out a way to make this work for both of us without making me feel like I was freeloading off of you."

"Auntie, I love you too. You've been like a mother to me. Mom was always with Dad or off doing the things she loved. You were the one who was always there for me. Did you hear about Scott having security cameras installed at the studio?"

"I did. It makes sense Jackie. I feel awful that I didn't put them up before. We might have caught the person who did that heinous thing. Now we may never know. I heard you met up with Rocco this morning."

"You did? Who told you?"

"Betty was in town to pick up a library book and saw you in the diner. Hard to keep a secret here. What did the two of you discuss?"

How much should I tell Ruth? My curiosity put her in danger last night. She deserved to know more. "Well first off, it wasn't a secret meeting. I've agreed to help Stuart and Kim. I'm not alone in believing she didn't do this. Yet she's been charged with a crime."

"While the real murderer is doing what, Jackie? I'm

sure Jeff told you to let them do the leg work after what happened last night."

"He did."

"But you're not listening?" Ruth asked.

"Not true. I am being careful and that's what I was meeting Rocco about. He was able to provide information to me that I didn't have. The people who hired him are part of an investment group. They wanted eyeballs here on the progress of the resort. I took a chance that it was Alan that he was watching. And I was right."

Ruth shook her head. "Jackie, the girls and I are having fun with Rocco. He's nice and makes us laugh. But be careful…he might not be what you think."

"We Parker women think alike. Jeff is checking him out for me. I'm not just acting on what Rocco is telling me without verifying his background story. But now Ruth, I've got to check back in with Stu. He was going goofy with Kim locked up. So, I gave him something to research for me. He used to be an investigative reporter…it's in his blood."

"Yes," Ruth said. "I knew that. Just be careful Jackie."

"I will. Enjoy your potluck dinner tonight!"

"What are you doing for dinner?"

"I thought I might grab a late bite at that brewery. Your meals looked so good there last night."

. . .

The text message from Stuart was waiting for me when I got back in my car. I hurried over to his office and looked over the work he'd done.

"Very impressive Stu. You've been busy."

"There's so much at our fingertips now. In years past I'd spend hours in the courthouse searching for documents. This would have taken days to do."

He quickly showed me where Jeff's list and his research intersected. Now he said, "I know you don't owe me an explanation as to the importance of this, but I'd love to hear one if you have time."

"And Stu, believe me I'd love to give you one. But it's probably better that I wait until tomorrow morning. There are one or two more steps to take. In fact, Stu, I'll need to go to the Stone Mill tonight. Might you be able to come with me? I don't want to be noticed or hit on," I laughed.

"As an attractive single woman, I'm sure you would be. Kim has a late-night appointment at Val's, so I'll be picking her up, but I'd be free for an hour or so."

"I'm glad to hear she's getting back to normal," I said.

"It's a start. But she didn't want to go during regular hours and have to face questions from others."

"Understandable. Can we meet there at 8:00?"

CHAPTER TWENTY-ONE

It was getting dark by the time I made it to the Stone Mill Brewery. They did a nice job with low lumens lighting shining down. Inside the place had a nice comfortable vibe to it. It was a younger crowd than the Wildwood Supper Club though, and I was glad to have Stuart with me.

Stu and I stopped to say hello to Mandy and Matt Drake who sat at a table looking out on the old riverside docks. They expressed their concerns for Kim, and Stu thanked them.

I was glad to see Pete wasn't working behind the bar tonight. His questions last night about me being the one buying the business, and why I needed to talk to George, seemed antagonistic.

Stu and I picked a small high-top table near the bar

and the bartender came over to take our order. Stuart ordered the Log Driver IPA, and I picked the Pulp Man Red Ale. "Thank you for asking me to join you tonight. I haven't gotten to enjoy these craft beers yet."

"Did Kim mind you getting out while she was at Val's?"

"No, she encouraged me to. I think I'm starting to annoy her, hovering over her too much. I'm sensing the old fighting spirit is returning. Val's manicurist agreed to meet her there after hours too, and Val is going to give her hair a trim. She's getting her armor in place to go back to work tomorrow."

The manager stopped by to say hello. "That waiter you were looking for last night is here now."

"Which one is he? I brought the things he left behind so I could give them to him this time."

The manager pointed George out. He was waiting on Matt's table. "Do you want me to let him know you're looking for him?"

"No, I'll just catch him before we leave. You don't need to interrupt him now."

"Say, aren't you Stuart Walters, the editor of the Harmony Hills Happenings? You did a nice article about us when we first opened. In fact, we framed it and put it on the wall. I wish I'd had you autograph it."

Stuart beamed. “Thank you. I’m glad I finally got here to enjoy the place. It looks great.”

Before the manager left our table, he told the bartender that our beers were on the house. That gave me an idea.

“Stuart, do you know Mandy Drake?”

“The gal we just met? Not really. Why?”

“I don’t know if you’ve heard but I’m buying the Parker Photography Studio from my aunt and Mandy is going to work for me.”

“I hadn’t heard! I guess I’ve been in my own little world. That is very exciting news. Now I’ll do that interview with you not only as the famous Jacqueline Parker, but as the new owner of a business in town.”

He seemed to have regained some of his usual vigor. Was it the beer or the excitement about his work?

“Maybe I should work the family business angle. That Parker Photography is staying in the community and in the family. With the protests against all the new places opening up and changing the face of the town, I think this would be a better approach,” Stuart said.

“Were people upset when this brewery opened too?”

“Not so much because they moved into this old long-abandoned building. It had become an eyesore. This end of town is enjoying some new life now.”

"Wanda told me that Shorty didn't seem to mind the competition," I said.

"I recall him even speaking up at one of the endless open mic nights at the Village Hall. He called out the opponents to the brewery's permit application saying the new place would be good for Harmony and that he planned on being the first to add their beers to his tap lineup. That really helped them get the necessary paperwork through."

"But back to Mandy."

He said, "I know Matt Drake. He used to do our yard work when he was a young boy. He's involved with his dad's business now, isn't he?"

"Yes. I'm using Drake Construction for the remodeling I'll be doing at the studio."

"They are the top construction company in the area. Local boy makes good success story there."

"I'd like to send them a drink or dessert, but I'd like you to do the ordering. The waiter is up at his station now. Can you catch his eye and wave him over?" Stu's questioning look demanded more of an explanation from me. "I'll explain later."

The waiter came to our table. "Sorry sir, the bartender serves this area," George said. "Shall I get him for you?"

"No. I wanted to get that young couple you're

waiting on a drink or dessert on us. Can you do that please?"

"I'd be happy to. Who shall I say ordered it?"

"Just say Stu and Jackie."

Here's where I caught an opening. The waiter wore a name tag, so I didn't have to explain how I knew his name. "George, I think I know a friend of yours, Lynn, the bartender at the Wildwood Supper Club."

"I don't recognize that name," he said.

"Hmm…maybe I misunderstood. She said you bought raffle tickets for her at the fundraiser on Saturday."

"I bought some for a group that Pete, our bartender here, pulled together." George gave a nonchalant shrug. "Well, if you'll excuse me."

"I see. She was just so excited about winning. And I think one of the other tickets won but we couldn't make out the phone number on it. You see, I'm working with the committee and we're trying to track down the raffle winners. Do you know who that might be? I have the ticket here if that refreshes your memory." I had come prepared with a raffle ticket with an illegible phone number written on it.

George took a quick glance at it. "That's not my handwriting. Sorry I can't help you."

"Oh goodness. Excuse my poor eyesight." I pulled out a copy of the list of raffle winners and took a look at it.

"Look I'm sorry, but I've got to get back to my tables. Hope you find your winner."

"I do too. The evening ended so suddenly with that murder. The committee was left scrambling to wrap things up." I laid down the paper and began rummaging through my purse.

I'd given Stu an additional task, and he took his cue, my kicking him under the table, like a pro. "Didn't I see you there that night George? Weren't you a waiter at the event?"

"I was. Look I've really got to run. The boss is giving me the eye."

"Here they are. Are these yours?" I pulled out the stapled-together series of five tickets.

George was obviously shocked. "Where did you get those?"

"My dog discovered them at the base of a trellis standing under a window at the Harmony House. I have a hard time imagining how they got there."

CHAPTER TWENTY-TWO

George quickly left our table and disappeared into the kitchen. He didn't come out for several minutes. When he did, he had a tray laden with food for another table of four. After he'd served them, I watched him move to Mandy and Matt's table. They looked in our direction and waved.

George passed by our high-top table and said that they'd ordered the dessert special and they had thanked us. He took a deep breath. "You obviously found those raffle ticket stubs in an odd place. I can explain. Would you be able to meet me on my break in half an hour? We could meet on the old loading dock out back."

I agreed.

Stuart however reminded me he had to leave to pick up Kim at Val's. "I would be more comfortable if you didn't meet him alone, and I'm not even sure what it is you're hoping to accomplish with this man."

"I'll be fine. This whole place is lined with windows looking out at that dock area. Nothing nefarious is going to happen. I just want some answers from him about what happened that night. I think he may have witnessed something that could help with Kim's case."

It was closer to an hour before George got his break. Stuart was gone, and so were Mandy and Matt, having left after stopping by to thank me for the dessert.

When I noticed George leave to go outside, I grabbed my drink and my purse. The manager saw me and reminded me the dock patio wasn't yet open to the public. "Is it okay if I just step outside to look at it?"

"Of course, but please stay inside the lit area. There is construction going on and I wouldn't want you to take a tumble," he said. "Plus, the staff has been using it as a smoking area. I will have to break them of that once we're open, so accept my apologies for the smoke smell."

"Thanks. I shouldn't be long. I imagine it's getting a little chilly."

George was one of those smoking waiters who used this area. He sat on a short concrete wall just out of the circle of light that came from the new fixture installed on the exterior stone wall.

"This will be a lovely patio area once it's completed," I said.

The dark river silently moved past on its way to the lake. Under the still surface it flowed with quiet power, just as it had for thousands of years.

"What is it you want, lady?" George said without further ado.

"Were these yours?" I opened my hand to show him the stubs.

"Yes, and now I suppose you want to know how they got by that trellis. Not that it's any of your business but I must have dropped them there when I went out for a smoke. The breeze would have blown my smoke over the patio, so I decided to move to a different spot. I must have ended up where you found those."

"It wasn't a big deal to me. I'm just having to account for the prizes, you understand. But we'll figure it out. Sorry if I upset you. That whole evening was upsetting. Did you know the murder victim? There are so many rumors swirling around about her."

"No…I didn't know her," he mumbled, taking another drag on his cigarette.

"Weren't you the waiter who spilled the champagne on her dress? Her ranting and raving could be heard above that snazzy music the combo was playing. What a drama queen she must be. I mean really, to raise a ruckus like that!"

George stood to pinch the end of his lit cigarette between his fingers to put it out. "That was me. The broad in the red dress was the lady who was killed? I didn't know that. Yeah, she was pretty pissed. I didn't even cause the accident. She backed into me. But she got all worked up, swearing she'd have my job, and did I know how much a dress like this cost. Geez, she went off."

"I've heard that about her. And that she had lots of enemies. People let a little power go to their heads. Did you see her later? Had she calmed down?"

"Why do you ask?"

"Luella Hagge was her name. Does that ring a bell for you? I thought perhaps you recognized her. Your family's business was involved in a civil suit with her as the attorney for the plaintiffs. Do you think she recognized you?"

I'd hit a nerve. Now what would happen? I could make out George's clenched jaw. He flipped his cigarette butt over the ledge and into the river. "Thought she looked familiar. That was a long time ago. Water under the bridge."

I was right. He didn't deny the connection.

"I don't think she recognized me. When I cooled down, I tried to find her. I didn't want to lose that side gig with Darlene. I ended up going upstairs after the two ladies in red went up there. I hoped to get to apologize to her."

"Understandable, George. Did you get to talk with her?"

"Yeah. I had to wait around though. She sat down in one of the closed off rooms and the other red dress broad left. Then this old dame goes in and I hear her reaming that Hagge woman out. I gave up. I wasn't supposed to be up there. But someone was using the back stairs to the kitchen, and I ducked into another room to wait until the coast was clear. Then through a crack in the door, I watched a guy go in the room."

His story works so far. That must have been Hannah and me using the back stairs and Betsy would be who he called an old broad. "Do you think the guy you saw go in the room was the murderer?" I asked in a conspiratorial tone.

"Could've been. I snuck a peek, and they were arguing. She took a swing, and the guy grabs her arm."

"Wow. Could you identify the guy for the police?"

"No, he had his back to me."

"You know George, I was on the landing when the

lights went out and a woman fell down the stairs. Were you still up there then?"

He was trying to hold his story together. He'd gotten so far into the lie that he couldn't find his place. He stepped closer to me. With his cigarette breath in my face he said, "I don't remember. I don't think so. I must have just left."

"I see."

He stepped even closer to me. "That's right. I left. I wasn't up there. I was back in the kitchen when the lights went out."

The last clue was in my pocket. I had to push one more time. But dare I? The smart thing to do would be to go back inside for safety and report this to the police. But then the scent of a good Cuban cigar reached me. I felt in my pocket, wrapping my fingers around a small plastic bag. "George, I hope you'll try harder to remember. This could be important to the case."

We stood in the shadowy part of the dock now, his menacing stance obvious even in the dim light.

"You were up there then, huh?" he said. "Now it's my turn to ask you...what did you see? Did you see the murderer?"

"I'm looking at him." I reached in my pocket and pulled out the piece of white shirt with blood stains on it.

"Why you little..."

CHAPTER TWENTY-THREE

A cold beer never tasted so good as the Stone Mill Brewery's Pulp Man Red Ale I held in my hands.

Luckily for me George had pulled back from giving me a shove that might have sent me toppling into the cold water of the Wisconsin River. It only happened because Rocco stepped out from behind a pile of lumber and said, "Excuse me sir, but you seem upset. Is there something wrong here?" He made a point of having his suit coat open to reveal his shoulder holster and the gun in it.

George stood there stunned when he saw we weren't alone and the short man next to him was armed.

"Rocco, how nice to see you. I love the smell of a

good Cuban cigar, don't you, George?" I said. Needless to say, I didn't expect an answer.

Rocco said, "You've got good taste, Jackie. They smell much better than those nasty cheap cigarettes you're smoking, George. You know you really should quit. It's a bad habit."

My phone had begun ringing…perfect timing!

The police arrived shortly thereafter, and read George Adamos his rights, arresting him for the murder of Luella Hagge. He was in a police cruiser on his way back to the station at this very moment.

Rocco and I had quickly decided drinks were in order.

"I was surprised to see you, Rocco…but very happy! What are you doing here tonight?"

"Your aunt called me. She asked me to stop in here as she thought you were going alone and was worried. But when I arrived you were with someone and I didn't want to intrude. So, I tucked myself in a corner and had a tasty Rueben sandwich. Delicious. I'd order it again."

"Good to know you didn't starve. That person was Stuart Walters. Our local newspaper owner, editor, and reporter."

I turned to the third person at our table. "How did you end up on the patio? You were certainly a welcome sight."

"That's nice to hear. I got done with my meeting early and thought I'd surprise the kids. But they'd left. I know the guys doing the work here getting the patio ready for summer, so I decided to check it out," Scott said.

"That flashlight beam surprised us. I'm glad you spoke Jackie's name, so I didn't feel I had to cover two people."

"Sorry about that. I didn't expect to see anyone out there. Much less three people with one of them being held at gunpoint. And then in the middle of all that drama Jackie's phone starts ringing!"

Rocco and I both started laughing.

"You should have seen yourself, Jackie. You looked from me to Rocco and went, should I answer it?" Scott said. "And Rocco says only if it's law enforcement. And you look at the caller ID and said it is!"

"It was awkward for a few moments while we listened to one end of your conversation," Rocco said as he took a sip of his iced tea. "I have my weapon drawn on a man I don't know. Scott here is shining a flashlight on us. People are gathering up there at the windows of the restaurant to see what's going on. Until finally you hung up and say the police are on their way."

"What was Chief Mathis calling you about? Just asking for a friend," Scott said with a grin and a wink.

"Jeff called to tell me that some prints I'd had him run matched a name on a list of employees who worked with Darlene the caterer on Saturday. He asked why I wanted to know about her employee's missing uniform shirt. I quickly told him to meet us here as soon as he could, and he would find out why."

"I saw you show George that piece of white fabric in a baggie. Was that what you took out of the vine earlier today when I held the ladder for you?" Scott asked.

Rocco leaned back in his chair watching us. "I have to say, you are both losing me. What's with the piece of fabric?"

"Now that's interesting. On Sunday, my dog Libby had to do her job."

"Do her job?" Rocco asked. "I'm sorry, never had a dog. What does that mean?"

"It means she had to go to a doggie bathroom aka outside in the grass. We were at Harmony House. I took her around a corner…doggie privacy. She finished up and was digging under a vine and came up with the stubs of five raffle tickets stapled together. They are for the purchaser to verify the numbers on the tickets he bought. The numbers sequence included my birthdate, so it stuck in my mind. Just a few minutes earlier I'd been at a window that was left ajar. I closed it but noticed the ivy climbing up a trellis to it. I just figured some other vine, like a moonflower, had ended up creeping in on the ivy. At the time it wasn't of special note, but...days later it all became part of this crime."

Rocco said to Scott, "Her aunt said she was observant, I'm learning just how much."

"And all because a dog had to potty," Scott said. "Now tell us why you ended up going back to climb up my ladder and get that white flower."

"As I now know, it wasn't a flower. It was a scrap of fabric. And you may not have noticed, but it has drops of blood on it. I believe they will get a DNA match with Luella. But if not, the fingerprints on the window ledge above the window match his."

"And that would be the window ledge in the room where Luella was murdered," Scott asked.

"No, the bedroom next to it. You see, that sitting room where Luella was asked to wait for Alan Morris to meet her in was part of a suite of rooms. The three rooms included a pink bedroom and a powder room that also had a door to the hall and was being used by guests. The pink room was Eleanor Harmony's bedroom when she was growing up. At the Historical Society meeting on Monday, she mentioned that the trellis, a sturdy and tall one, was used by friends sneaking in when she was a teenager."

"By friends I'm assuming those of the male gender,"

Rocco said. "I think I'd like to meet this Eleanor woman."

"She's one of a kind. But to your question, yes, boys. I was already trying to find other suspects to help Kim Walters' case. I need to thank you Rocco, for confirming that Betsy Bennett had ample reason to take out Luella, and so did Alan Morris. And I've been checking into both of those people. I've even considered Len Lampert, her current opponent. But as I learned more about Luella, especially from Stuart's Tuesday morning article in the newspaper about her past dealings, I considered that another person who would have a motive could have come from further back in her past…from the years she litigated. Then Kim's arrest happened that same morning and I felt even more urgency."

"I'm thinking when I saw you here at the Stone Mill Tuesday night you already wanted to talk to George. Why him?" Rocco asked.

"Before my friend Wanda and I got here that night a couple of things came together. I'd seen the list of raffle winners. One was Lynn, a bartender at the Wildwood Supper Club. Her prize was won from one of my birthday sequence tickets lying at the base of the vine. She directed me to here, the brewery, to find the guy who purchased that pack of tickets for others. He was at the event as a waiter. At that point I was just curious as to how the ticket stubs got there. Then not three hours later, I get a rock thrown through my window with a threatening note attached."

"So that was last night. What went on today that got you to the point of what just happened?" Scott asked.

"After the rock throwing incident, Jeff, Aunt Ruth, and I stayed up talking. Neither of them felt Kim did it. Alan Morris and Betsy Bennett were possible suspects, but I had this suspicion about it being someone who'd been wronged by Luella in her time as an attorney. She had engaged in some high-cost lawsuits and Stuart's research provided a list of them. We also had a list of people who bought tickets and were at the event, and the police interviewed them. But we didn't have all the names of the wait staff from Darlene. Some had left early as the party was winding down and just the auction and raffle drawings were left. This morning Jeff got those names for me and Stuart compared them to lawsuits Luella had been involved in. The nexus was George Adamos. He was at the event and involved in a case Luella tried against a family delicatessen in Greensville. The entire family business was ruined, over a batch of bad potato salad."

"That case sounds familiar. The circumstances seemed to point to the buyers not properly refrigerating the salad. But in the civil case the jury found the Adamos

Deli liable and the monetary judgement against them was the largest in memory."

"That's the one. It was George's family business."

"I remember you dashing over to the house this morning and using my ladder to get the fabric down. You wouldn't tell me what you knew," Scott said. "Now I get it."

Rocco asked. "They've already confirmed the fingerprints then? I would suppose his prints were on file in the state because of licensing requirements. So, he came into your radar as a suspect. You already had two suspects who you knew were on the second floor during the time frame…Kim and Betsy. Kim told the detectives about Alan, but no one saw him. I'm still unclear how you came to the conclusion you did. Please enlighten me. I'm intrigued."

"The white fabric and the waiter's uniforms," Scott practically shouted out with pride. "Did I get it right?"

Rocco nodded. "I believe our detective Jacqueline has already verified with the caterer that the fabric you helped her capture from the vine matched the fabric of the wait staff's uniforms."

"Good one Rocco. But I didn't have time for that. I did however reach the caterer, and she confirmed that the shirt count was off when the laundry service picked them up. Fiber comparisons are on Jeff's to-do list."

"Now please continue, Jacqueline," Rocco said.

"I think that George was trapped in the sitting room with Luella when the lights went out. The lights came back on fairly quickly. I'm not certain when he actually did it, but since he had no reason to be up there, he didn't want to be caught and used the trellis to escape. He probably waited until the lights came on and everyone's attention was directed toward Kim Walters lying at the bottom of the stairs. Finding the ticket stubs in such an unusual place was a big clue. George tried lying his way out of it tonight, but the more I pushed and the deeper we got, he ended tripping himself up. Blood on his shirt was the final undeniable truth he had to face."

"Looking back at all of this it fits together," Rocco said. "I admire your powers of observation and memory for detail. I do however have to remind you to not corner a dangerous animal."

"You're right. I was about to leave and let Jeff handle the arrest in the morning when I smelled that aromatic cigar smoke of yours. Nice signal to let me push forward. How long had you been listening, Rocco?"

"From the conversation about the champagne spill. Did you know he was the waiter involved with that?"

"Ah no…I sort of fudged on that. I didn't know it was him, but I took a chance."

"And he confirmed it in spades. Well done, Jacqueline. Please let the authorities know that I'm available to testify to what was said if needed."

"I appreciate that, Rocco. Perhaps I'll see more of you this summer since this guy here is getting my new place ready."

We all left the Stone Mill Brewery at the same time. Another clean, clear spring night. I did a friendly shoulder bump against Scott. "Will the construction work be done soon? I'd like to enjoy a boat ride with Rocco and the gals."

Scott put his hand on my back as we walked through the doorway. "I am going to put it at the top of my long list, Jackie. Trust me, I'd like to see you back soon as well."

CHAPTER TWENTY-FOUR

The first person I wanted to call on Thursday morning, after enjoying the deviled eggs Ruth left for me, and before I hit the road, was Stuart. But he beat me to it. "I was worried about you after I left you alone at the brewery last night. Kim wanted me to call and make sure you were okay. Especially after that rock through the window situation. Did they ever find out who did that awful deed? One of the people you were investigating, perhaps?"

"I appreciate you calling. Things got a little exciting, but the outcome is that the real murderer of Luella Hagge is sitting in the jail cell now. And your attorney will be notifying you that charges against Kim will be dropped."

"Are you serious?" Stuart said, the shock coming through on the phone call.

"I certainly am, Stu."

"How can I thank you for trusting my Kim? We are in your debt."

"Stuart I'm just so sorry for what Kim had to go through. As to the rock thrower, I suspect it had nothing to do with my investigations into Kim's innocence, but rather a disgruntled unhappy bartender who is protesting the resort development coming because they fear that people from the big cities, like me, are going to change Harmony. I wish I could tell him I'm actually a local gal returning home."

"And I for one, and I believe I can speak for my wife as well, are grateful you are coming home and look forward to having you be part of our business community."

I wasted no time in going to the police station. My late night handing off of George to the law would seem to settle things. But before I left, I wanted to verify that he would be locked up. I have empathy for the man and his family and what they lost. By most accounts of the Greensville deli case, the attorney Luella Hagge pulled out all the stops to not only put the screws to the deli, but to dramatize the plaintiffs' misery to the point of absurdity. She garnered her clients a large financial settlement of which she would receive a large portion. But all those thoughts were lost in the fact that he murdered a woman. Was it in a rage? I'm sure it was not premeditated, just the fact that the two of them were at the same place and same time. Did the champagne episode aggravate the situation? Had the timing of all the people in and out of that sitting room gone differently might he have walked away? Lights going out and Kim falling were distractions and he quite easily had gotten away on the trellis. It was the dropped ticket stubs, and the torn shirt that were his doing in.

"Jacqueline Parker, good to see again so soon," Jeff greeted me as I pushed the door open. "To what do I owe this pleasure?"

"I'm leaving in a few minutes and wanted to thank you for trusting me enough to help pull this together," I said.

"This is hard for me to say, but I don't think we would have made this arrest without you. I didn't mention it, but yesterday Lou, Detective Taylor, spoke to Senator Bennett, questioning him regarding a previous relationship with Luella. She based those questions on your getting the photograph from Patti revealing that he'd lied about knowing Luella. Now she's going to let them know that their private life will remain that because of the arrest of George Adamos. I'm sure they'll be relieved."

"Is Detective Taylor coming back here today?"

"Probably not. Why are you wondering about Lou?"

I smiled. "Just asking for a friend."

"Is Scott going to have the remodeling at the studio done soon? I'm expecting an invitation to the grand opening."

"I'm on my way to meet him now."

Scott waited at the diner. We were going to go over a few sketches and ideas he'd put together about the studio. I was pleased to see Ruth and Mandy there as well. There were part of this process and deserved a voice in it.

"Jackie, you should have told us what you planned. Matt and I would have waited last night," Mandy said. "You could have been hurt. I can't believe our waiter was a murderer. Why did he do that?"

Dolly came over with a coffee cup for me and a pot of coffee in the other hand. "Morning Jackie. You all ready to order?"

"Give us a minute, Dolly," Ruth said.

"I think his motive was anger at what he went through years ago. But he didn't plot to murder her. He had a lot of bitterness in him and cosmic forces put him and Luella in a place that proved deadly for her and almost as bad for him. Raw emotions were released. Now she's gone and he'll be locked up for a long time."

Dolly returned and took our order. Spring sunshine poured through the diner windows. Wanda walked into Val's Cut-n-Curl. I'd have to call her on my way out of town and let her know what happened. But Val probably would know all about it already.

Hannah's shop was open, with select pieces displayed on the sidewalk in front of the store. She'd probably hear about it soon as well. It would certainly be reported in Friday's Harmony Hills Happenings.

"Jackie? Jackie?"

"Sorry, I was just spacing out for a second. Yes Scott, what is it?"

"I've found that we have to keep the front windows as they were because of the Main Street historic district requirements."

"I'm fine with that. In fact, I like it. It'll be perfect." Change is good, but so is keeping things the same. Now I'll have some of each, old and new, with my Parker Photography business.

CHAPTER TWENTY-FIVE

Libby lay in the morning sun on the mat just inside the studio door. After much discussion it was decided I could take her back with me to my loft in Chicago. Construction would commence shortly, and no one wanted to risk her getting under foot and ending up hurt.

Ruth had the movers lined up. The changes in her cottage at Shady Pines could be done while she lived there. Ruth had always lived simply and frugally. She and the gals had already boxed her smaller personal things. She opted to take her furniture with.

"Don't you want to get a new couch and dining set?" I asked.

"I'm good with these. It'll be hard enough to leave, even though it's exciting at the same time. Bringing familiar things with me will make the transition more comfortable."

"I hope I didn't make you feel you had to do this. I wouldn't want to think I ran you out."

"Don't be silly Jackie. I am so ready for this. Doesn't mean it wouldn't be hard. I will miss being right here on Main Street in the heart of all the action. But I can't be in two places at once and now the place I most want to be in is a cottage among the trees, along the river, and with my friends."

"You know I never asked if you got any prints out of that film?"

She looked down at Libby and then reached to rub her behind the ears. "When do you think you'll be back?"

How strange. She just totally avoided answering me.

"I'm not sure. Why? You're all set to move out, aren't you? And remember Scott installed security cameras so the place will be okay with no one in it."

Ruth looked up at me with a sadness in her eyes. She almost spoke, but then Wanda knocked on the unbroken front shop window and walked in.

"Hey girlfriend, congratulations on solving the murder! Val told me the good news."

Hannah saw us and came across the street. "Wow! That arrest was sure a surprise. Glad that's over."

"Hannah, I owe you a glass of Cabernet. The woman in the champagne episode was Luella," I said.

"Oh my gosh, I forgot about that. I'll catch that wine on your next trip in. Will you start the remodeling soon?"

Ruth answered. "It's starting next Monday. And I'm on my way to Shady Pines and retirement happy times."

"Well good for you!" Wanda and Hannah said at the same time.

"Happy roads ahead," I added, watching Ruth's expression.

She smiled back at me and blew me a kiss like she used to do whenever I left for school, or to play with my friends. I knew it meant we'd talk later. And sometimes that's okay.

THE END

I'd love to have you signup to receive my newsletters. They give us both a way to interact and get to know each other.

Click to signup for Suzanne Bolden's newsletter

Every month I draw a winner from the new signups, to receive a free paperback from either of my series.

ABOUT THE AUTHOR

Here are a few ways to reach me...I'd love to stay connected!

Please sign up for my monthly newsletter. I'll share things about my life...both personal as Brenda Felber and professionally as my pen name Suzanne Bolden.

Like/follow Suzanne on her Facebook page

If you follow me on these two, you'll be automatically notified when new releases are available.

Bookbub

Amazon Author Central

Check out my website www.suzannebolden.com

Thank you for reading my books. If you enjoyed them, a review is much appreciated!

ALSO BY SUZANNE BOLDEN

Katie Murphy Cozy Mystery Series

#1 Pour Decisions

#2 Pick Yar Poison

#3 Raising Spirits

#4 Auld Lang Stein

#5 A Wee Lepre-Con

#6 Paws for a Pint

7 The Elf Did It

#8 Matrimony and Malice

#9 Read Between the Lines

ALSO BY SUZANNE BOLDEN

Parker Photography Cozy Mystery

#1 Captured on Camera

#2 Murder in a Dark Gloom

#3 Focus on Fraud

#4 An Appraisal to Die For

#5 A Filmsy Excuse

#6 A Negative Result

#7 Framed for Murder

#8 Digital Deception

#9 A Developing Attraction

#10 Skewered Perspective

#11 A Killer Shot

#12 Holiday Havoc

Series completed

www.ingramcontent.com/pod-product-compliance
Ingram Content Group UK Ltd.
Pitfield, Milton Keynes, MK11 3LW, UK
UKHW042003190726
13854UKWH00005B/2143

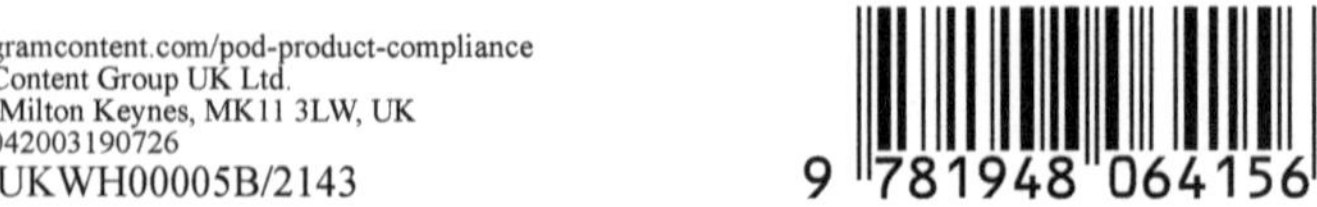